MILLENICA

It's a New America During a New Millennium

by David M. Cooper

PublishAmerica
Baltimore

© 2007 by David M. Cooper.
All rights reserved. No part of this book may be reproduced, stored in a retrieval system or transmitted in any form or by any means without the prior written permission of the publishers, except by a reviewer who may quote brief passages in a review to be printed in a newspaper, magazine or journal.

First printing

All characters appearing in this work are fictitious. Any resemblance to real persons, living or dead, is purely coincidental.

At the specific preference of the author, PublishAmerica allowed this work to remain exactly as the author intended, verbatim, without editorial input.

ISBN: 1-4241-8312-X
PUBLISHED BY PUBLISHAMERICA, LLLP
www.publishamerica.com
Baltimore

Printed in the United States of America

MILLENICA

It's a New America
During a New Millennium

Chapter One
The Idea

It was the end of summer, year 2010, and the nights were beginning to suggest that cooler weather was on the way. Shopping malls recovered from their back to school sales and stores filled empty shelves with Halloween costumes, candy and decorations making a formal announcement that the holidays were on the way. Busy parents put away their picnic gear, fishing poles, and swimwear as they placed their summer memories into artistic gold and silver picture frames and digital family photo albums. They nestled back into their boring daily work routines while their children returned to school. At Boise State University, the hallways filled with a sense of enthusiastic energy. While future professionals checked their class itineraries to ensure they selected the right courses needed to achieve their predetermined degrees, Richard Weeks was having a difficult time accepting his class curriculum for the semester.

"Joey, we have to do something about this," said Richard.

Joseph Sweet was sitting on the campus lawn under a large maple tree looking at this lunch inside the paper bag he picked for the day. Joey knew Richard wouldn't survive the monotone droning of his political science instructor, Professor Simon Girswald.

"About what?" asked Joey. "Oh, yeah, you got old man Girswald this semester. If we includes me, then let me get my shovel so I can start digging you a grave. I can see your obituary now, death by boredom."

"What were my parents thinking," asked the fashionably dressed, twenty-three year old college junior, "me, a political science major?" His Ray Ban sunglasses protected his eyes from the sun. ""Don't they realize the President of the United States makes less per year then Bill Gates? Isn't it clear that the salary of a mayor, governor, or senator doesn't come close to the income of Donald Trump?" Richard was stretched out on an antique university bench, directly across from Joey, who was devouring a ham and cheese sandwich, and appeared to be more interested in his lunch than what his friend was saying.

Richard sat up and continued, "Employment depends on votes. Votes take time and money, and that's money wasted if you lose the election. Actually, if you listen to all the political parties, you'll notice that they're promising to do the same things, only better. In the end, the winner is the one who's better looking, has the most money, and doesn't allow anyone to visit the skeletons hidden in their family closet. Who cares if they're qualified, just as long as they say what everyone wants to hear."

Joey came up for air from his lunch and said, "Just like being at a party. Maybe that's why we use that word." He got up, and started dancing in front of Richard. "Life is just one big old party. It's a Democratic Party, two to the right. It's a Republican Party, two to the left. It's a Communist Party, kick ball change, and that's what we call the Political Party System, tah dah." Joey took a bow, then stopped dancing and looked at Richard seriously.

"You know, I don't remember wearing a funny hat, throwing confetti, or drinking champagne the last time I was hired for a job."

"You're right, but it's protocol when someone wins an election," laughed Richard. "Party, party, party, it's no wonder nothing gets done quickly in this country. All our elected officials are too busy partying."

Richard's tone changed when he thought about his destiny ending up in the hands of the voting public. The possibility of being a politician made him sick. To make matters worse, he had to take a class that was being taught by a dinosaur that should have been fossil fuel a long time ago.

"I'm going to do it," said Richard. "I've completed the majority of my electives. All I need to do is change my major to business or economics."

Joey got down on one knee, eye level with Richard and said, "Now you know your parents won't go for that, and you know you won't last a day without their purse strings tied around your arms and legs."

Joey was right. Richard had to do what his parents wanted because they were funding his entire education as well as his expenses. Mr. and Mrs. Weeks were creating a small empire in the timber industry. Together, they managed a combination of log trucks, lumberyards and paper mills, and with all empires come power. To maintain their power, they would need political support. They were grooming their only son to become a lobbyist, and to do that, Richard would have to attain a degree in the field of politics.

Richard had a different plan. He agreed to attend a local university and would move to the Ivy Leagues to further his education. His plan was to get into Boise State University with his parent's assistance, complete his electives, get a job to finish his education and graduate with a degree in business. However, somewhere along the way, Richard forgot the most important part of his plan, to get a job. He didn't want to start at the bottom and work his way up. Being the only child in a progressing timber empire, Richard was used to the finer things in life. When he was little, he thought he was his favorite comic book character, Richie Rich. His golden blond hair and bright blue eyes allowed him to do so, and as an adult, Richard had grown into a modern version of his comic book mentor. He liked living the lifestyle he was living. The lifestyle his parents were maintaining. Nothing but name brand clothes could touch his skin. Whether it be a university social function or a meeting with his professors, Richard's attire was fashioned to fit the occasion. University books and supplies were all new, nothing uses. His university co-eds became used to having at least one round of cocktails on Richard when he was out and about. To be big, you had to act big, and Richard didn't want to lose his status as the big spender on campus while he progressed through his university courses.

Joey got up, sat on the bench next to Richard and started thumping him on the head with his finger.

"Come on," he said, "use that head of yours for something more than a high priced hat rack. Think of a way to keep your parents happy and keep the money coming in. At the same time, use your political science education to create a career in business. If you can do that, you can do anything."

Richard was glad to have Joey as a friend. Some people thought he was a bit of a control freak, but Richard thought of Joey as being confident with leadership qualities. He was half Afro-American and half Native-American, which according to Joey made him All-American. This, added to his male model like good looks, made it easy for him to get dates on the weekends. Joey's dark sarcastic personality was the devil's advocate to

Richard's positive energetic attitude. Each time Richard came up with a blockbuster idea, he'd bounce it off Joey first. Being that Joey was a bit of a risk taker, he knew his ideas had a good chance of being accepted. However, also being cautious, he knew Joey would check every detail for flaws. The glue that kept their friendship strong was the love for competition. Life without it would be unexciting and tiresome. They both had a fascination for reality television. Nothing was better than sitting in front of the tube, picking a contestant and hope that individual would be the one to win a recording career, get off the island, eat the most cockroaches, finish first in a race around the world, lose the most weight, get the high salaried executive position, be the first down the fashion runway, or find true love. The more original the concept, the better.

"Besides, at least your parents see potential in you," said Joey. "When my parents heard I was going to major in communications, they immediately cast me as an anchorman for the evening news. Thank God I'm not parent whipped like you. My parents understand that because I have a job and pay for most of my education, I make my own decisions. They can give advice, but I call the shots."

Joey thought about the cable station where he worked.

"You know, even though it looks run down, my boss told me at one time he had big plans for that old cable station. He eventually wanted to expand and create half a cable station and half a television station. He has the equipment in storage to make it happen, but he doesn't have the financing to keep it going. That's why I'm there. Eventually, I'm going to own that place."

Looking at his Gucci watch, Richard realized how late it was getting.

"Whoa, it's five to one," he said.

"Crap, we'd better get going," said Joey as he discarded the remains of his lunch-to-go in the trash receptacle across from the bench. "You have a date with Griswald and I have an advanced public speaking class to attend. By the way, where is the advanced public and why do they want to speak to us?"

Richard looked at Joey for a second and then started laughing. They both were walking towards the main building when Richard said, "You know Joey, you may have something there."

"What, did I forget to zip up again?" Joey fussed with the zipper on his jeans.

Richard looked at Joey's crotch and then rolled his eyes.

"Smartass. No listen," he said. "You told me to use my political science major to create a career in business. I've got an idea that just may do that. It all depends on Griswald's class."

Joey stopped and looked at Richard. "You came up with an idea already? What is it?"

"I hear Griswald makes his students do a political science project and it's seventy-five percent of the final grade," said Richard.

"Okay, and?" asked Joey impatiently.

"As a project for this semester, why not create an election that's similar to a reality TV show? It'll have competition, eliminations, drama, the works," said Richard.

"A reality election?" Joey sounded confused, but smiled like he found the idea intriguing.

"An election reality TV show," replied Richard. "Contestants will have to perform their campaign promises in front of an audience. The audience eliminates anyone who can't perform their promise from the show. I don't have all the details worked out yet, but what do you think?"

"I like it," said Joey. "Tell you what, let's both think about this overnight and bang heads tomorrow during lunch."

"Sounds like a plan," said Richard.

The two classmates ran to their next class energized and enthusiastic. The concept was clear, follow the rules of political science and then do some math. Keep the political, subtract the science and then add business. Take a boring subject and turn it into something fun and exciting. This semester, Professor Griswald's political science class would go down in university history.

Chapter Two
The Ratings

She and her assistant sat in the overstuffed corporate office waiting room chairs. She suspected there was trouble, but not to the point of meeting with the corporate network director of programming. This year's television lineup wasn't bringing in the ratings, and her show, *The Gallery*, a reality show about artists, was one of them. The concept seemed exciting. Take a group of inspiring artists, have them perform various artistic acts to win $100,000 and become the owner of a New York art gallery. To everyone's surprise, by the middle of the season, rating analysis indicated that the show was a dud. The public wasn't interested in watching drama queens paint theme murals on the side of California suburban homes. They switched channels when they saw amateur artists trying to create designer furniture from recycled materials. They thought it was ludicrous that mature adults would create a rain forest of silk plants for endangered stuffed animals. No, this time, her magic wasn't working, and the executive producer feared she had lost her touch.

"Ms. Kendrick, Mr. Soars will see you now." The secretary's

polite smile greeted both Janet and Robert as they got up to enter the lavish office. Janet wasn't sure what to expect, and she came prepared. Robert would assist with a formal presentation if it came to that. Usually, her wit, charm, and sophisticated personality got her out of most bad situations, but this time, she knew it wasn't going to be that easy.

"Janet, how the hell are you?" rasped the middle aged corporate director. Years of cigar smoking had taken a toll on his throat. Frank Soars patted Robert on the back and said, "And who do we have here?"

"Forgive me Mr. Soars," replied Janet. "This is my new assistant, Robert Garcia. I asked him to join me."

"Good afternoon Mr. Soars," said Robert as he eagerly shook the network director's hand. "You can't imagine how honored and excited I was when Ms. Kendrick requested I join her." Robert continued shaking hands as he gushed on. "I mean me at the corporate office, meeting the corporate network director in person."

Janet politely interrupted, "Robert, I'm sure Mr. Soars knows how important he is." She reached out and released the vice grip he had on her boss's hand. "Mr. Soars, you wanted to see me?"

"Uh, yes," said Frank as he took his hand and shook it a couple of times to get the blood circulating again. "Let's sit over here at the table." Frank allowed Janet to lead the way. He never tired of looking at her hourglass figure. For a woman of thirty-six, Janet could still turn heads. Her brunette hair and dark brown eyes made her look a little like a young Elizabeth Taylor. She went to sit, but Frank stopped her.

"Here, let me get that for you," he said. He pulled her chair out and smiled as he watched her firm round bottom snugly fit in the seat. Being a bald, slightly overweight, fifty-five year old married man with one heart attack behind him, Frank took advantage of every simple sexual pleasure he could get. Robert waited for him to pull his chair out, but Frank quickly sat down directly across from Janet to savor the bird's eye view slightly plunging neckline. He looked up at Robert and gruffly said, "Sit down Mr. Garcia. We don't' have all day."

"Yes, Mr. Soars," replied Robert and he awkwardly sat in his chair.

"Janet, I'm going to come straight to the point. Your show is stinking up the ratings. I've never seen such a catastrophe in the thirty some years I've been in the business." When it came to business, Frank Soars didn't care if you were male, female, animal, vegetable or mineral. He'd let you have it with both barrels loaded.

Janet's worst fear was becoming a reality. Her career had peaked and it was downhill from this point on. Her Midas touch was coming to an end. She was doing everything she could to keep Frank from saying that dreadful word, "cancellation." Robert quickly lifted a briefcase to the table and pulled out a bundle of graphs and analyses reports as Janet started her presentation.

"Mr. Soars, if we make a few adjustments here and there, things will change," she said. "In these reports, I've outlined what could happen if we just change..."

"Janet, there's not going to be any adjustments. Your show is being cancelled." Frank's words flew from his mouth like a boxer's right hook, hitting Janet square in the face.

Robert sat in disbelief. How was he going to explain this to his wife? She'd carve him up and serve him for dinner if he came home and announced that he'd just been fired from his new job. She warned him not to get involved with television, or as she put it, that fickle industry of unstable occupations.

"Mr. Soars, no!" begged Janet as her female ego started crumbling.

Frank stood up and said, "I'm sorry Janet, my hands are tied." This was his way of saying the meeting was over. Robert placed the reports back into the briefcase.

Janet made one final attempt to change his mind, "Frank, you've got to give me another chance. You've seen my work and you know what I can do. I promise, I won't let you down. I can do this."

"As a matter of fact young lady, that exactly what I'm going to do." Frank put his hand on Janet's shoulder and walked her to the door. "Listen, everyone gets a bad egg every now and then, and no matter how much you paint the damn thing, it's still going to stink. Get rid of it." Frank stopped at the door and looked Janet directly in the eyes. "You're right, I do know you. I've been watching you progress through this industry and you've done some excellent work for this network. Until now, your reputation was spotless. I've convinced the network brass that you can redeem yourself and you've been given that second chance. Understand?"

"Yes sir." Janet wondered what the network brass said about her.

"Good, you've got six weeks to come up with a new idea. That's about how long it should take us to get rid of that rotten egg of yours. Now, go work your Kendrick magic and bring us back something fantastic." Frank looked at the ceiling, smiled and then said, "Artists, they can be so temperamental. This is going to be fun."

"Thank you Mr. Soars," Janet said humbly. She walked from the office into the waiting room and then stopped. She was looking straight ahead as if in a trance. Robert closed the door to Franks' office and almost ran into her when he turned. He could see she wasn't herself and tried to get her attention.

"Ms. Kendrick, are you alright?" he asked. "Ms. Kendrick?"

All of a sudden, Janet sprung to life as panic and anxiety coursed through her. She grabbed Robert firmly by both arms and said, "Did you hear what he said? Six weeks! Six weeks to come up with a fantastic idea. I'm supposed to create another reality television show from scratch during the holiday season? Where do I start?"

Seeing the distress in her eyes, her loyal assistant replied, "Well, maybe we should go back to your office and then we'll create a new game plan. You know how these walls have ears." Robert smiled at the secretary, who was looking directly at them. He'd gotten Janet to release her grim, took her by the hand and led her to the door. Janet was mumbling incoherently as he escorted her from the waiting room to the hallway outside.

"That's it, back to your office, and when we get there, we'll talk about you possibly taking a small vacation." Robert wasn't sure what he was doing, but it seemed to be working. Janet was nodding her head yes as if Robert was coming up with some great idea.

"That's it, a vacation for Thanksgiving," said Janet. "Go visit my family for a few days and clear my mind, get my thoughts together."

Chapter Three
The Class Project

It was the beginning of November and Boise's cold wet weather was right on schedule. Simon noticed how it affected things so differently. Mother Nature created works of art, while humans cringed in pain, and his arthritis was proof of it. Through his classroom window, in the distance, Simon saw a group of maple trees. Their colorful leaves blurred together like a painter's pallet showcasing splashes of gold, yellow, orange and red, while others were scantily dressed revealing only bare limbs. As he looked out the window, he could see his reflection. He didn't recognize the pale, thin old man wearing glasses looking back at him. How many years was it now? Had it been over forty years since he started his teaching career? He turned from the window and looked at the room. The building had been renovated a couple of years ago, as well as the distinguished style of his classroom. The majestic oak wood desks, the dark jade green marble floor, and the antique crown molding that he admired so were gone. They had been replaced with colorful plastic desks framed in chrome, ordinary beige tile floors, and simple white plastered walls. Simon felt like he was going to be the next thing to be replaced.

He also noticed the number of students attending his classes was diminishing as the years went by. Was it he, his style of teaching, or was it the trend of the future? When he was going to college, to enter the field of politics meant you were creating an opportunity to change the world. You were on your way to leading the country. Perhaps it started after the assassinating of his mentor, President J.F. Kennedy, or maybe Watergate, or the impeachment of President Nixon. Now it seemed that students were taking political related courses to find out why the American government was such a mess. They didn't ask how they could influence a specific culture to create peace. Nor did they want to know how they could improve the economy. Everything was why this and why that. Why are we running out of Social Security, and why are we attempting to revise it if it isn't useful anymore? Why has the U.S.A. fallen so far into national debt? Is our government setting the example for Americans to spend beyond their means? Why did we sell nuclear arms to third world countries? Didn't that offset the balance of power and ruin our standing as being the number one nation in the world, and by doing so, didn't that United States inflict terrorism on itself? They questioned every theory and concept, and Simon felt like he had to constantly defend the topic he loved so much.

Simon gave out a deep sigh. He had run his course and wanted to pass his baton to the next worthy contender in the human race. In one more year, he'd be able to retire. Like his classroom, things had changed so much from when he was a young man, and perhaps his way of thinking had become obsolete. He constantly doubted himself, but wouldn't admit it to the faculty or his students. Around the world, things were changing at an alarming rate. Technical innovations outdated themselves within a year.

Were his students right? Was political diplomacy being replaced by the power of big business? From the frustrations of his students over the years, Simon could sense something was about to happen. Business and government would have to join forces and redevelop to advance our nation. The millennium needed an innovative administration to create a modernized political philosophy. Just like the political pioneers of his decade, or further back to the pilgrims who settled this country, he knew there had to be a natural progression towards a new way of leading. Simon wanted to teach a least one more year, in hopes to find his apprentice. To find and nurture the student who wanted to create a new beginning for this country. His dream was to assist in creating a future president of the United States. Through his teaching, he desperately wanted to be a part of it. This would be his way of making a difference in the world.

"Professor Griswald, I believe we had an appointment?"

Richard Weeks was standing at the door. Simon had forgotten that he wanted to meet with the young man to discuss his political science project.

"Oh yes, come in Mr. Weeks. I wanted to talk to you and go over your class project in more detail." There was something about Richard that bothered Simon. It wasn't so much his perfect designer look, or his effervescent attitude, but for someone majoring in political science, when it came to assignments and projects, Richard acted too elusive and vague.

"My project, certainly, what do you want to know?" replied Richard.

"Basically, from what I've gathered, you're spearheading your own election?" asked Simon.

"That's right, what else do you want to know?" Richard knew he had gone as far as he could with avoiding Simon's inquiries, and his election would be going on the air soon.

"What is the purpose of this election?" inquired Simon. "How are you presenting it? Who is your target audience?" Simon thought for sure this would be the last time he had to question the boy. He was finally going to get a straight answer.

"Professor Griswald, please have a seat." Richard escorted Simon over to one of the bright plastic desks and then walked to the front of the class giving the appearance that he was about to give a class presentation. "Picture an election, like no other election in university history. What would make this election different, no, superior to other elections?"

Simon looked unimpressed and grew tired of his student's classroom showboating. "I'm sure you're about to tell me Mr. Weeks. That's why we're here."

Richard cleared his throat and continued, "Currently, elections are based mostly on campaign promises. Each candidate is elected through a voting system based purely on trust. If a candidate can convince an audience that they are the best to lead, by utilizing promises, they eventually will get the votes. In the past, candidates had different ideals, each with opinions that differed from each other. Currently, all candidates are promising the same thing, which leaves the American public with little to choose from, other than their loyalty to their political party. This is becoming a reoccurring problem with our current electoral system, causing elections to end in virtual ties."

"Mr. Weeks, that's an interesting observation, and what is your solution to this reoccurring problem?" asked Simon.

Richard walked up, placed both hands on Simon's desk, leaned forward, looked him straight in the eyes and said, "What if we put those candidates to the test?"

The professor leaned back a bit, startled and replied, "How do you plan to do that?"

Richard stood straight with a huge smile on his face. "We do it by making the candidate perform tasks similar to the promises he or she makes. If they fail to perform, they lose their audience's trust, lose their votes and will be eliminated as a candidate."

In all his years of teaching, Simon never heard anything like this. Richard wasn't describing an election, it sounded more like a game show.

"Mr. Weeks, what you're explaining is a bit unusual, no completely abnormal. How do you plan on presenting this bizarre election?"

"I'm glad you asked," replied Richard. "I have a friend who works as an assistant editor for a local cable station. He presented my project to his boss, who thought it would make an excellent program for the university students. We began production three weeks ago, and the show airs tomorrow at four o'clock. Since this is going to be my project for your class, I'd like you to see it."

Simon sat dumbfounded, and began to break into a cold sweat. All he could do was stare at Richard, speechless. The words "production" and "airs" kept running through his head. Had Richard made it known that this was a Boise State University project for his political science class? Did he mention Simon's name? The Dean had approved nothing. What if he sees it? How was he going to explain this?

"Did you say this airs tomorrow?" Simon stated the sentence all in one tone.

"That's right, at four o'clock. Professor, I can tell by your response and expression that you may be a little apprehensive, but there's no need to worry. Everything was done professionally and in good taste." Richard had played his hand and now it was a matter of keeping the game going.

Simon regained his senses and wanted to make sure the young student knew the ramifications of what he'd done.

"Richard, I'm positive your standards of good taste and my

standards of good taste differ immensely," he said and his voice increased in volume as he spoke. "Did you know that anything regarding the university, aired publicly, has to be approved by the Dean first? How am I going to explain to him that I didn't know one of my students was putting his class project on television? Mr. Weeks, you've put many things in jeopardy, which includes my retirement next year as well as you chances of graduating from this university."

"Professor, don't worry," Richard said calmly. "I promise everything will be fine. You and I, we'll think of a way to smooth things over with the Dean. Shoot, I bet once he sees the election, he'll recognize you as the creative figurehead that you are. One who allows his students to think outside the box and quenches their thirst for knowledge. The kinds of stuff great educators are made of." Richard sounded like he was selling used cars.

No matter how much Richard reassured him, nothing could make Simon feel at ease with what was about to happen tomorrow at four o'clock. One thing was for sure, he had to make it a point to watch Richard's election. He had to be able to defend himself from all embarrassing accusations. He had to know what to say when the Dean called him into his office. Then again, this was a show for college students. Simon's only hope would be the public's lack of interest. Perhaps a simple class election wouldn't be worth watching, especially one as bizarre as this.

Chapter Four
Clearwater Cable

Clearwater Cable was running at an all time high. In its twenty-two year history, never was there such a response to a television program like what was happening today. The small cable company had to purchase additional telephones and extensions as well as hire temporary staff to handle the incoming calls that would soon be flooding the lines. Dale Brophy breathed a sigh of relief feeling confident that he'd made the right decision hiring his new assistant editor, and because of it, the company had an upswing in cable orders. The company owner remembered what it was like before Joey was hired. The feeling of despair knowing that the company he was creating was being considered a candidate for bankruptcy. It worried him, knowing that the banks that placed their trust in him now looked at him as a risk because the money just wasn't coming in. Dale believed that with the success of this show, and possibly more like it, he'd have additional orders for cable installations, perhaps get his company finances out of the red and then begin working on his next venture, creating a television station.

Brophy walked out of his office and looked around for Joey. As he scanned the room, he saw something he hadn't seen in a long time. It was the look on the faces of his employees. They actually appeared to be in high spirits. You could even say they were happy as they busily prepared themselves for the day's magical event. Their energy enveloped Dale and he acquired a buzz from their enthusiasm. He wanted everything to run smoothly, and a final meeting with Joey was in order to go over the show's outline.

"Joey! Hey, Sweets, where the hell are you?" he shouted.

"I'm over here Mr. Brophy." Joey was in the corner of the room drinking coffee, going over the day's program schedule. He just finished his checklist on operations and procedures and had one last detail to go over before the show went on the air. Joey had to make sure there was enough time scheduled for callers to cast their votes and have all votes calculated by the end of the day. According to his schedule, everything was in order and it should be a smooth show. Dale walked over and sat himself across from Joey and then asked if there were any problems he should know about. Joey handed him a copy of the schedule.

"Everything is under control," he said. "If all goes as planned, this show will be a complete success. My friend Richard just called from the university and said they have quite a crowd gathering in the recreation area."

This was music to Dale's ears. Capturing a younger clientele meant longer cable contracts and he smiled as he went over the schedule. Besides creating business, another thing Dale like about Joey was the way he paid attention to details. He spotted problems in advance and made sure they were eliminated. In other words, Joey got things done efficiently. He also knew that Joey was doing a lot more than what he was being paid to do. As an assistant editor, Joey was practically running things. By all rights, Joey's title should have been station manager.

"Joey, I want you to know ho much I appreciate what you're doing for this company." Dale kept his eyes on the schedule while he spoke.

"No sweat, Mr. Brophy. All I do is run things, I'm good at that. A lot of places don't even listen when you're the new kid on the block. I should be thanking you for letting me do the things I do." Joey meant what he said and was having fun making things progress for the cable company.

"Well, I just want you to know that in a few months, you and I will be talking promotion. You've done a lot for me and I don't want to lose you." This time, Dale was looking directly at Joey.

"Hey, I'm not going anywhere. I like this place too much," said Joey. "Besides, I just found out I have a promotion to earn, and this show today is just the beginning."

"I just hope we get half the response you're predicting," said Dale.

"From what Richard told me, he's one hundred percent sure of his prediction," said Joey. "He's put a lot of work into this project over the last three weeks, and it sounds like most of the college campus will be watching and participating. My job is to make sure we can handle all the calls and get the numbers out in time."

Joey put down the schedule and he and Dale observed the activity within the cable station. They both smiled, but for different reasons. Dale was happy seeing life spring back into his company. There was light again at the end of the tunnel. Joey was glad that he was making a difference for Dale and at the same time, was assisting his best friend with his college project.

Chapter Five
Destiny

Janet walked into the local pub and thought it didn't look too bad. Even though it had the smell of wood oil and stale beer, it was clean and had somewhat of a charming atmosphere. It looked like it used to be a log cabin at one time and all its large wooden furniture remained because it was just too heavy to remove. There were a couple of pinball and video machines against the back wall, a pool table off to the side, a few tables on the lower level covered with red plaid tablecloths, and green leafy plants in all the appropriate places. There appeared to be ten to fifteen patrons in the establishment, all within their twenties. Janet made her way to the dark oak bar and noticed the cut of the wood looked as impressive as the bartender behind it. Not a bad place indeed, she thought as he approached the bar. Janet always had a thing for the lumberjack types, and the snug fit of his jeans and his tight red flannel shirt made her remember how long it had been since she'd slept with a man.

"Good afternoon. What can I do for you today to make those beautiful dark eyes of yours light up?" said the chiseled barkeep.

Janet was a bit surprised at the bartender's bold approach, but was flattered at the way he was flirting with her. This kind of behavior was common in the clubs of California, but things had obviously changed in her hometown. With a brazen smile, she replied, "You can start by making me a gin martini, straight up with two olives please."

"I like a woman who knows what she wants," said the bartender as he prepared Janet's drink. "Let me guess, you're not from here?"

"You're half right. I grew up in the outskirts of Boise and moved to California about ten years ago." Janet leaned forward and then cooed, "Why, is it that obvious?"

The bartender laughed as he positioned the gin martini in front of her. He leaned forward and folded his muscular arms on the bar. He was directly in front of her and his hazel brown eyes gazed deep into hers.

"Well, let's just say you don't fit the description of the type of person who visits this place," he said. "We get mostly the university types in here. You look a little more established and doing quite well I might add."

Janet started swirling her finger around the rim of her martini glass. This guy is good, she thought.

She leaned forward to look at his nametag and then reached out and shook his hand. "Thank you, Jake. I'm Janet, and as for doing quite well, that's yet to be determined."

"Oh, don't tell me there's trouble?" said Jake as he leaned against the back bar cabinets giving Janet full view of his physique. He was definitely giving her signals.

"That's why I'm here," replied Janet. "My boss gave me this project to complete in six weeks. That was three weeks ago and I'm no closer to having it completed than I was then. We thought it would be a good idea if I came home for Thanksgiving and visit my family, you know, to take the pressure off and get my thoughts together."

"We?" inquired Jake.

"Oh, I'm sorry, that would be Robert, my assistant," replied Janet. "Actually, it was his idea. He's a nice guy, but a bit on the shy side. I like him, he's loyal and he doesn't question anything I ask him to do. He's a very good assistant." She finished the martini and gestured for another one.

Jake placed the second martini in front of her.

"This Robert, will he be joining you?" he asked.

Janet took a drink and started feeling toasty inside as the alcohol made its way to her bloodstream.

"No, he's back in California waiting for me to come up with a miracle," she said. "It's just me and my family. Jake, I need a miracle to happen in three weeks. How much longer is it until Christmas?"

Jake looked at Janet with a devilish grin and said, "If it'll make you feel better, I have a Santa suit at my place. Christmas could come early this year. You and I could make our own miracle happen."

Janet thought about Jake's offer and probably would have taken him up on it if she had one more martini.

"What about Mrs. Clause? Wouldn't she get upset if she found out you were stuffing someone else's stocking?" she jokingly asked.

"There is no Mrs. Clause," replied Jake in a husky voice.

Seeing the direction the conversation was going, Janet thought it would be a good idea to change the topic. Things were moving a little too fast and she needed to concentrate on an idea for a new show. She turned around and looked at the pub. There were more people, a lot more. As they came in form the cold, they gathered in front of a big screen television located adjacent to the bar.

"Jake, why is this place getting so crowded?" she asked.

Jake's fascination with Janet made him forget to keep track of the time. It was almost four o'clock and today was the day of that election show the students were talking about for some time now, and he promised they could watch it on his television.

"Damn, I'm sorry, it's almost show time." Jake ran over and turned on the television, receiving a round of applause from his customers. Janet got up and walked over to the television. She wanted to see what this show was that was causing such a commotion.

Back at the university, the same thing was happening. Simon let his class out early and was quickly walking to the student recreation area where the election was being shown. He hadn't slept and was a wreck, worrying what was about to happen. Today, it was the talk of all his classes. His students went on incisively about it. How could he have been so blind to what was going on? The Dean, who was in his office, probably watching the program, would question him for sure. Simon reached the recreation area and turned the corner. He stopped in mid stride and stared at the crowd ahead of him.

"Oh my God," he said, almost fainting.

It was wall-to-wall students and faculty. Simon pushed his way into the mass to get a better view of the television.

"Professor Griswald! Professor Griswald, over here!" It was Richard frantically trying to get Simon's attention.

"Yes, Mr. Weeks." Simon's voice was shaking as he moved closer to Richard.

"Look at all these people. Can you believe it?" said Richard.

"No, not really," replied Simon. "Richard, I'm hoping you were discrete with your information. Like I said yesterday, this should have been approved by the Dean, and with all the attention it seems to be receiving, I'm a bit concerned."

Simon's thin frame was being tossed to and fro. Richard had to reach out and grab him at one point to keep him from falling.

"Professor, look at all these people and think about why they're here," said Richard. "They're here to participate in an election. That itself should make you happy. Now why the large turn out, that's what you're about to find out. Get ready to see an election like no other election you've ever seen before."

Back at the pub, Janet was amazed at the energy in the room and the amount of people interested in what was about to happen. She turned to the bar and asked, "Jake, what's going on? What is this?"

Jake was busy taking and preparing drink orders chaotically being given by the university students. While he was pouring beer from the tap, he managed to give Janet a rundown of the events to come.

"Well, from what I've heard, the university is holding an election to determine who will be the next class secretary, treasurer, and president. The thing is, in this election, the candidates have to do things on TV and the students vote based on how well they do."

"Things, what kind of things?" asked Janet. Her attention went back to the television.

"I don't know, but I think we're about to find out," replied Jake.

All faces turned toward the big screen television and the students at the pub became quiet. Janet returned back to her barstool as Jake served the last of his orders. He returned back to the bar as not to block the view of any of his patrons, stood next to Janet and placed his arm around her claiming his territory for the evening.

Janet was oblivious to Jake's advances. She sat staring at the television anticipating what was about to happen. She felt her

Midas touch returning and her gut feeling told her that she was in the right place at the right time. Perhaps it was the martinis making her feel so good, but Janet knew this was the miracle she was waiting for.

The gathering at the university recreation area calmed down. You could hear the sounds of students whispering to each other as they made themselves comfortable. Richard was proud of the fact that he was responsible for creating this class election craze, but in the back of his mind lurked a dark depressing thought. What if his peers looked at this project as a joke and he loses his university credibility? He'd become a slave to his parent's wishes and end up living the life they had planned for him. Nobody could see it in his face, but Richard was just as nervous as the Professor standing next to him.

Simon was exhausted. He'd been surviving on coffee throughout the day to keep himself awake. He felt like he was watching his own train wreck, and there was nothing he could do to stop it. His tired old heart was pounding like he'd run a marathon. The Dean, the Dean, what am I going to tell the Dean, was all he thought about. Was this it for him? Were his career and his retirement going to be ruined by a student's class project?

Chapter Six
The Class Election

The audience consisted mostly of university students and faculty members. They were divided in half by a narrow walkway that lead to the stage where the six university class candidates sat to the right. The two candidates for class secretary sat in front, behind them were the two candidates for class treasurer, and behind them were the two candidates for class president. To the left of the candidates sat a large television. Below the stage, between the television and the audience was a podium that was accessible from the narrow walkway. Behind the audience were two long tables covered with white tablecloths that held computers and telephones manned by volunteers who sat patiently waiting for the election to begin. The audience was told to get ready and the announcer readied himself as the countdown began.

"We're on in five, four, three," the stage director counted the last two numbers on his fingers and then pointed at the announcer who immediately burst into action. He ran down the narrow walkway to the stage, turned and faced the audience.

"Good afternoon everyone, and welcome to *Class Campaign 2010!*" he shouted. The audience replied with cheers and whistles. "This is the election you've all been waiting for, so let's get this show on the road. Here's the man who's going to put you all in the driver's seat, please give a big round of applause for your campaign host, Richard Weeks!"

Richard came running from the back of the audience down the narrow walkway to the podium. His new dark blue Armani suit told everyone that he was much more than just a television show host. His audience welcomed him enthusiastically while he bowed to them and then to the candidates. When everyone settled down, he turned and faced the television camera.

"Wow, you guys are great, thank you. First, let me start by explaining something to our television audience." Richard looked around, leaned forward toward the camera, motioned for it to come closer and then spoke softly like he was telling a secret.

"This election was filmed earlier this week. That's how all of us can magically be in two placed at one time." He gave a wink and then suddenly stood straight up and started talking with an energetic bold tone.

"But, that shouldn't affect the outcome of this election. As a matter of fact, our studio audience is going to be playing an important roll today. They will be demonstrating how the voting process works, and we expect you to follow their lead. It's simple, all you need is a telephone to participate." The camera panned the audience as Richard called out, "Hold them up if you got um!" The audience cheerfully showed off their cellular phones.

Richard turned, faced the stage and greeted the candidates. They all replied in their own ways. Some said hello, others smiled and waved, and some just sat there without a response at all. Richard turned back to the audience and continued.

"These ambitious individuals are the focus of our attention

this afternoon, because you're going to be voting for them. It will be up to you and our television audience to determine who is best suited for the position of class secretary, class treasurer, and class president." Richard turned and gestured toward the large television up on the stage.

"Isn't she a beauty? We want you to watch this television very closely. It's the story teller that will guide you through our election today. All the stories will begin the same way, once upon a time there was a candidate. It will give you valuable information that you will use when it's time to vote. Now, all our candidates were asked to give their reasons why they should be elected for their prestigious student class positions. As expected, their promises were pretty much the same. So, instead of giving you candidates who can talk the talk, we made them walk the walk for you." The audience started murmuring. "That's right, nobody gets away without performing in this election. When we come back, you're going to see just how well your candidate can keep a promise, but first, let's take a small commercial break. We'll be right back."

The commercial ended and it was on with the show. Richard welcomed everyone back and continued where he left off.

"First, we'll begin with our candidates for class secretary, Andrew and Jeremy." Richard looked up at the two candidates with a smile.

'Hello gentlemen," he said.

"Hello Richard," said both candidates at the same time.

Richard started reading from a card he held in his hand, "Let's see, during your campaign for class secretary, you both stated that you would keep operations running smoothly and organized. You would support your leaders and assemble meetings when needed. You would accomplish assigned duties and create a calm controlled atmosphere. Am I correct?"

Andrew and Jeremy both agreed.

Richard turned, looked at the audience and said, "So, what kind of task could we create that's similar to these duties? Why not a day in daycare? Think about it, who would need support, organization, and a calm controlled atmosphere? A daycare facility with twenty toddlers between the ages of three and seven, that's who, and to test their assembling skills, let's make it more challenging by having our candidates create a field trip to the park. It sounded like a good idea, so we did it. Let's see how smoothly these two candidates kept things running."

The lights dimmed, Richard gestured toward the large television and then said, "Once upon a time, there was a candidate named Andrew."

The segment started with a daycare representative advising that the candidates were being monitored to ensure the safety of the children. The candidate's behavior and relationship with the children were also being monitored to determine how well each individual would handle the demands of their leader.

Andrew approached the children individually and introduced himself to them as if they were adults. Some looked at him and drooled, while others started crying. This spurred on giggles from the audience. Andrew didn't have a plan of action, so by mealtime, it was obvious that he was running into trouble. Some children were scamper about screaming and screeching while others were throwing things at each other. Andrew was holding two crying three year olds as he ineffectively ordered the children to sit down and eat. Some of the audience felt sorry for the crying kids and others laughed at the scandalous ones screaming and making a mess. The field trip to the park was next, and this was where Andrew really showed his lack of organization and poor assembling skills. He managed to get all the children to the park, but he left two behind on the way back. The responsible daycare representative who stayed behind shook her head and claimed the two children. By the end of the segment, Andrew looked exhausted, and everyone could tell he was glad the assignment was over. He was embarrassed, apologized to the representatives, and gave a list of excuses for his lack of performance. The segment ended and the television went dark.

The lights remained dim and a spotlight shined on Richard. He gestured to the television again and said, "Once upon a time, there was a candidate named Jeremy."

Jeremy entered the room making funny noises and carrying a bunch of colorful balloons acting like a birthday party clown. He handed each child a balloon as he asked them their name and told them he was Uncle Jeremy. The result, he gained the children's full attention, causing the audience to laugh at his antics, but respect his creative ability of taking control. Prior to his assignment, Jeremy prepared a system to keep track of the children for the field trip. He turned it into a game and practiced with the children before meal time. He called it *The Park Buddy Game*. The children were paired off and assigned a buddy. Each time Jeremy called out, "Find your park buddy!" a timer was set and the children scurried about laughing and looking for their assigned partner. Once found, they would hold hands and form a double conga line. They worked at it until they managed to get it down to four minutes and the kids had a great time. During mealtime, the children had decorated Jeremy with their lunches, but he did have them sitting on the floor eating their meals. The representatives snickered at times, but they were impressed with how well Jeremy was handling their group of children. On to the field trip and *The Park Buddy Game* worked out so well, that the daycare representatives included it into their daily procedures. When his assignment was over, he hugged his munchkin family, and as he left the building, the children and the daycare representatives all waved goodbye.

The audience cheered and gave Jeremy a standing ovation and then the lights came back up and Richard took over.

"Okay voters, now it's time to do your thing," he announced. "Make your decisions based on your candidate's performance. To vote for Andrew, dial CLASS AN (252 – 7726). To vote for Jeremy, dial CLASS JE (252 – 7753).

The studio audience immediately started dialing in their votes, and the telephones behind them began ringing. The volunteers answered all the calls and input each vote into the computer system, which was automatically tallying all the votes. To make time for voters and money for Clearwater Cable, Richard took another commercial break.

The university students at the pub and recreation area began dialing in their votes. Most were surprised at the poor performance of Andrew, who was the favorite candidate before the election. He looked and acted like the better candidate, but like the saying goes, actions speak louder than words. They judged his lack of performance and poor leadership ability. Some even made comments on what a loser he was and they were glad they got the opportunity to see him in action. Needless to say, Jeremy was winning by a landslide.

Clearwater Cable took the sudden tsunami of incoming calls and they quickly input voting information in their computer system. Clearwater employees felt the pressure, but enjoyed the challenge and they liked being part of something original. Dale couldn't believe what was happening as he watched the action at his cable station. He contemplated the possible partnership of Brophy and Sweet. Joey was busy running from place to place making sure everything and everyone was under control. He stopped for a moment to take a breath and smiled. He wished Richard could see what was happening and wondered what his best friend was doing at this time.

At the recreation area, Richard watched the students as they started dialing in their votes. He listened to their comments and knew his class project was a success. He could stop worrying about his parents and he laughed at the strange feeling he was getting watching himself on television, being part of his own audience. He turned and looked at the expression on Simon's face, but to his surprise, there was no expression, none at all.

Simon didn't know what to think. Nothing bad or embarrassing had happened. There was no mention of him or this being a class project. As a matter of fact, as unusual as it was, the election was going quite well. However, it wasn't over yet and there was still plenty of time for something to go wrong. Suddenly, Simon thought of something else, since this was being aired on television, how far did it reach? Where else were people participating in this election?

Janet ordered another martini as she watched the election. She started to relax knowing her wish for a miracle had come true. The response from the students as well as their voting frenzy made it clear that this was the new show she was looking for. She made herself comfortable in Jake's arms as she watched the rest of the program. She looked at him and gave a wink, suggesting that he might be temporarily wearing his Santa suit for her for the beginning of the night.

After the commercial, Richard welcomed everyone back and the show continued. Andrew and Jeremy had left the stage and it was time for the treasurers.

"Hello ladies," said Richard and both candidates replied.

"Everyone, please welcome our two candidates for treasurer, Emily and Sasha. Both candidates were asked why they should be elected for class treasurer and during their campaign they stated that they would be held accountable for cash, credit, and all financial transactions, as well as keep clear accounting records and have statistics and reports available when needed. Is that correct ladies?"

Both Emily and Sasha nodded their heads.

Richard turned, faced the audience and smiled. "So, what was our task for these two candidates? How about make them cashiers at Boise's own *Universal Foods Grocery Store?*"

The audience made concerned comments and ooohing sounds.

"Oh, it sounds like some of you shop there, and you know how hectic things can get and how long the lines get to the cashier counters," he said. "It doesn't matter, it sounded like a good idea so we did it. Let's see just how accountable our candidates were."

Richard turned, gestured toward the television and said, "Once upon a time there were two candidates named Emily and Sasha." The lights dimmed and everyone watched the big screen.

During this event, both Emily and Sasha worked the same day at different counters and were fully clad in the familiar *Universal Foods Grocery Store* uniform. Store representatives explained that both candidates were following the same store procedures and would have professional cashiers to assist when needed. Duties included collecting cash and coupons as well as making change, weighing fruit and vegetables and calculating prices, implementing senior citizen discounts, collecting food stamps, and making credit card and debit card transactions. At the end of their shift, it would be announced who balanced their cash drawers, made the least mistakes, and offered the best service with a friendly smile.

Security cameras were used to watch the candidates and monitor line progression to both counters. Two small portable cameras were strategically placed to capture the customer's reactions as well as the cashier's performance.

The day began and the grocery store opened its doors.

Customers flooded into the aisles. The portable cameras captured the candidate's surprised expressions as the mob entered the store. Customers made their selections and made their way to the cashier counters. At the same time, people continued to enter the store. Both Emily and Sasha started out needing quite a bit of support from their assisting store cashiers, but as time went on and the lines progressed, they both seemed to catch on to the store procedures at the same speed. Actually, the store cashiers were surprised at how well the girls were handling things and dealing with their customers.

The candidates performed very well at the counter and offered professional and friendly service as well as learned the store procedures as if they were regular employees. It was clear that this was going to be a tough decision based on performance.

It was time for Sasha and Emily to count their cash drawers, balance their money, and turn in their paperwork. Their assisting cashiers escorted them to the counting rooms to act as witnesses. While they were being escorted, Emily inquired why she needed a witness. The assisting cashier explained that it was an accounting procedure to keep things fair between the candidates and to ensure their paperwork was correct.

Sasha counted her cash drawer and everything she took in and handed out balanced with her paperwork, except for her cash. She was short by one dollar and twenty-three cents. The store cashier told her not to worry, that for one day's work, she did an exceptional job.

Emily counted her cash drawer and like Sasha, everything she took in and handed out balanced with her paperwork, except her cash. She was over by exactly one hundred dollars. The store cashier acting as witness thought this was a bit unusual and suspected there was a mistake. Emily acted nervous and made a strange comment suggesting that she had made more money for the store. The store cashier recounted the items in the cash drawer and found that there was a void to a credit card for exactly one hundred dollars. A customer had changed his mind and wanted to pay in cash. The credit card report showed the void was made, but the charge to cash was not done. Once the charge to cash was completed, Emily's cash drawer balanced perfectly. The store cashier reminded Emily that in the future she pay more attention to her paperwork.

The television went dark, the studio lights came up and the audience was very quiet. Richard looked at them with a suspicious expression.

"You're thinking right now aren't you? That's good," he said. "Okay everyone, it's time to pick your class treasurer. To vote for Sasha, dial CLASS SA (252-7772). To vote for Emily, dial CLASS-EM (252 – 7736)."

The audience started talking quietly amongst themselves. Richard turned to the cameras and said, "I think they need a few more minutes, so let's take this time for a commercial break. We'll be right back."

The response at the pub and recreation area was the same as the studio audience. Conversations went on between university students and it appeared that Emily's ethics and honesty were being scrutinized.

PUB: "Sasha was short, but not by that much and she did get a good review from her store cashier."

REC AREA: "Emily balanced, but she sure looked nervous. It was like she didn't want the store cashier to be there with her."

PUB: "What was that comment about making one hundred dollars for the store? Yeah right, that was for the store."

REC AREA: "You know, she could have pocketed that one hundred dollars and nobody would have known. It wasn't recorded on her paperwork."

PUB: "There were two things about the counting room that Emily didn't know. She didn't know she was going to be on camera and she didn't know she was going to have a witness."

REC AREA: She was probably waiting for the right moment to pocket the money. She wasn't expecting the store cashier to recount her cash drawer."

PUB: "Most people would have apologized or made a comment about it being a dumb mistake, not a profit for the store."

REC AREA: "More money for the store. More like more money for Emily."

Students started dialing in their votes, and due to her questionable actions, whether intentional or not, Emily did very poorly.

The commercial break was over and Richard welcomed everyone back. Emily and Sasha had left the stage leaving the two candidates for class president. Richard looked into the television camera and reminded everyone that they still had time to vote for class secretary and class treasurer, then he turned and faced the audience.

"The time has come to elect your class president," he said. "So, at this time let me introduce your two remaining candidates. Everyone, please welcome Margaret and Jonathan." The two candidates expressed a half hearted smile.

Richard looked at them, then at the audience and continued. "Yes, well, your candidates were asked why they should be elected for the honorable position of class president. During their campaign, they both stated that they would accept the responsibilities of class president and lead by example. They would listen to their fellow students and would follow through with programs needed to improve the university as well as deliver services to meet the student's needs." Richard looked at Margaret and Jonathan and asked if this was correct.

Both candidates hesitantly agreed, then Richard turned and faced the audience again.

"What task could we arrange that would put these candidates in a place where they had to listen to what was being said to them and be held responsible for what they were told, as well as following through with their delivery?" he asked.

The audience began to murmur.

"What, can't you figure it out? Your candidates were put to work in a pizzeria. This included taking orders as well as delivering them. This was a good task and the outcome is interesting. I'm anxious to see how our voters respond. Let's watch and see how well our candidates listened and delivered."

The lights dimmed and Richard gestured to the television as he stated the familiar phrase, "Once upon a time, there was a candidate named Margaret."

To keep thing fair during this task, Jonathan and Margaret were to work at the same pizzeria, but on different days. They were shown the procedures for answering the phone, taking orders, and making deliveries. When making deliveries, they could either utilize their own vehicle or use the standard scooter issued by the pizzeria. No uniform was needed, but they did have to wear a logo jacket when making deliveries. The candidate offering the best service would be determined by the number of correct orders and the number of deliveries.

Margaret started her shift dressed in tight designer jeans and a thick white sweater that fit snugly in all the right places. Her shiny blonde hair was put up in a long ponytail giving her that perfect college sorority girl look. Margaret definitely dressed for the camera as well as for the male viewers. Her first two orders came at once and were from a group of husbands watching football in different neighborhoods. Margaret handled the order taking procedures well and she asked all the right questions regarding sizes, toppings, beverages and side orders. At the same time, she smiled at the camera as she flirted with the happy husbands. Her orders were given to the cooks and then were prepped for delivery.

Margaret didn't have her own mode of transportation, so she utilized the company scooter. She put on the pizzeria jacket, loaded up the scooter with both orders, and was on her way.

There was one problem. Margaret was not familiar with the suburban outskirts of Boise and she assumed she would be given a map or someone would ride along with her, but this was not the case. All she received were two addresses, so her first stop was to a gas station convenience store to purchase a map. Margaret parked her scooter in the parking lot, took off the jacket, placed it over her orders, and then entered the store. Little did she know that in the car next to her were two very hungry preteens, who just happen to be in the mood for pizza. While Margaret was in the store, the kids helped themselves to a couple pieces of pizza from each box. They put everything back the way it was and placed the jacket back over the boxes making them look totally undisturbed. After she purchased a map and received directions, Margaret returned to the scooter and was on her way. She forgot to put the pizzeria jacket back on and it fell to the street about a block away from the store. The audience was thoroughly entertained witnessing the mischievous children stealing the pizza and now this.

Margaret's first address was close to the convenient store, so she made it there in good time. Not realizing the jacket was missing, she took the orders to the door and rang the bell. A big burly guy wearing a football jersey answered and greeted Margaret with a big smile.

"Well now, I see the pizzeria is stepping up the quality of their delivery staff. Aren't you a pretty little thing?" Margaret responded with a shy sexy smile and handed him the deliveries as well as the receipt for the bill, which was paid for by credit card. She thanked him for the business, was about half way to the scooter, when all of a sudden, they guy called her back.

"Hey, what's the deal? You get hungry on the way here of something?" The man showed Margaret the box with the two pieces missing. She was not amused and told the guy to stop playing games. She accused him of taking the pieces himself in order to get a discount or even a free pizza. He said he was going to call her manager and she told him to do so.

She returned to the scooter and that's when she realized that the pizzeria logo jacket was missing. She remembered placing it over the boxes at the convenient store, so she headed back the way she came. She found the jacket in the middle of the street a block and a half from the store. From a distance she saw that it had dark tire marks and was torn. She parked on the side of the street to further inspect it. A tattered pizzeria logo jacket was not planned for her wardrobe budget, but she realized that she might have to pay for the thing.

Next, she checked the second order to see if it was still hot. She opened the box and to her surprise, she saw two pieces missing. The look on her face was priceless and it hit her that the guy was right about the other order. She tried to arrange the pieces so it would look like a whole pizza, and in doing so, she got pizza sauce all over her fingers. She unconsciously wiped the sauce on her white sweater, leaving bright red finger marks on her, well let's just say, in the most inappropriate spots. Margaret also didn't notice that due to blowing in the wind, her shiny blonde ponytail was now a mass of snarled twisted hair.

The studio audience, the students at the pub and at the recreation area were all laughing out loud at this point. Margaret sat on the stage looking totally embarrassed.

Worrying about her customer complaint, the torn jacket, and her second uncompleted pizza order, Margaret checked her map and headed to her second destination still not aware of the red marks on her white sweater. She reached the address, took the delivery to the door and knocked. She was not greeted with a smile like at the previous address. This time, the guy just stood there, wide eyed, staring at Margaret's sweater.

She looked down and saw the inappropriately placed red stains.

Margaret screamed and dropped the pizza box as well as the rest of the order letting it crash onto the front door landing. She turned, ran back to the scooter and drove away leaving the husky homeowner standing and staring, with a pile of pizza at his feet.

Everyone watching thought Margaret was putting on an act and they couldn't stop laughing. This looked more like a situation comedy than an election.

Margaret put the traffic torn jacket on to cover her finger stained sweater before she returned to the pizzeria. The condition of the jacket made it difficult to button or zip, and the front of her sweater was left slightly exposed. She knew she had a lot of explaining to do and due to the bad report from her first customer, the manager was waiting for her to return. Margaret immediately walked up to her to explain what happened.

The pizzeria manager took one look at Margaret's condition and couldn't believe her eyes. Wearing a dirty torn company jacket, hair in a mess, what looked like blood on her sweater, the manager assumed that the beautiful young coed had been sexually molested.

"Margaret, what happened? Who did this to you? Oh my gosh, was it that man who called about you? That beast, did he do this to you? Are you all right? Do you want me to call the police? That pervert, he's not going to get away with this. You poor thing, you sit down and let me handle this. Do you want me to call your parents?" The manager was pelting Margaret with questions so quickly, she never gave her a chance to answer.

The entire event had been filmed at a distance. The cameraman was still filming as Margaret was being questioned. The manager turned to the cameraman and yelled, "You must have seen what happened, is she all right? Did you get that bastard on tape while he did this to her?"

The cameraman smiled and said, "Yeah, I got it all on tape."

Margaret broke down in tears. She didn't know what to do, so she took off the jacket, dropped it on the floor and ran out of the pizzeria crying.

The segment ended with the camera on the pizzeria manager, staring out the door saying, "I'm going to call her parents. I hope she'll be all right." In the background, you could hear the cameraman chuckle and say, "Sweet."

Laughter roared from the audiences at the pub, recreation area and in the studio audience. Finally, the studio audience calmed down and the spotlight shined on an unprepared Richard, who had been laughing along with them and now was doing his best to regain his composure.

"Okay, okay, whew, I told myself I wasn't going to do that." Richard pulled himself together, gestured to the television and said, "Once upon a time, there was a candidate named Jonathan."

Jonathan started his shift wearing jeans and a Boise State University sweatshirt. He looked like an ordinary university student. His first call came from a woman who wanted three large pizzas and was very specific about what she wanted.

"It's very important that everything is correct," said the woman. "Now, listen very carefully. We'll have the Hawaiian pizza, extra pineapple and Canadian bacon. Please make sure there are no bell peppers on this one. Next, we'll have the vegetarian pizza, extra mushrooms and tomatoes, but absolutely no onions. Instead, we'd like to add pineapple. Next, we'll try your special taco pizza. Please make sure that half is mild and half is spicy. Did you get all that?"

Jonathan had to repeat the order three times until he got it right and scribbled it on a thin piece of scratch paper. Another call came and Jonathan placed the woman's order off to the side unaware that he laid the paper in a small puddle of water. The thin paper soaked up the water causing most of the writing to become blurry. Jonathan finished taking the second order and proceeded to place them on the order forms for the cooks. He picked up the scratch paper and saw that most of the order was impossible to read. The helpless look on Jonathan's face sparked laughter back into the audience.

Thinking to himself that this was only a pizza order, he could make a few mistakes. So, he did the best he could to repeat the order from memory. However, for whatever reason, Jonathan's short term memory was not performing well that day and a few of the items that were supposed to be removed, found there way back onto the pizzas. The orders were issued to the cooks, were prepped and ready for delivery.

Being the future university class president, Jonathan refused to use the company scooter. He borrowed a pickup from his friend Billy, and in return, Billy would receive one free pizza and a ride with Jonathan during deliveries. This was fine with Jonathan. At least he'd have someone to talk to.

They made it to the first house in less than twenty minutes. Jonathan delivered the pizzas, collected the money and returned to the pickup to make his next delivery. As they were leaving, Jonathan noticed Billy was staring out the window at the house.

"What's the matter Billy?" asked Jonathan. "Did I forget something?"

"No, we used to live next to that house when I was little," replied Billy. "The Hansons, they were strange. It seemed like someone was going to the hospital for one thing or another. That family is allergic to everything. One kid almost died. I think it was from bell peppers or onions. Anyway, all I remember is it seemed like there was an ambulance in their driveway at least once a month. The sounds of the sirens at all hours of the morning, that's why we moved away."

Jonathan stopped the pickup, looked at Billy and said, "Did you say bell peppers and onions?"

"Yeah, he almost died," replied Billy as he continued to stare at the house.

"Shit!" shouted Jonathan as he turned the pickup around and sped back toward the Hanson's house.

"Let me guess, you put onions and bell peppers in their pizza," said Billy without blinking an eye.

Within minutes, Jonathan was running up the walkway to the front door of the Hanson home. He pounded and rang the doorbell as he yelled, "Don't eat the pizzas! Don't eat the pizzas! Please open the door!"

Mrs. Hanson opened the door allowing Jonathan to burst into the room. Frantically, he looked around and noticed the family was sitting at the dining room table selectively dividing each pizza.

"For goodness sakes, what's the matter?" asked Mrs. Hanson.

"Don't eat that!" Jonathan ran over and shoved all the pizzas off the table. Some fell to the plush carpeted floor, some fell onto the laps of family members, and some flew across the room sticking to the designer wallpaper on the dining room wall.

Several of the audience members sat with their mouths wide open, shocked at what they were watching. Others were choking from laughter, their throats still sore from laughing at their first presidential candidate.

Jonathan explained the whole situation to the family as they cleaned themselves and stared at the mess around the room. He apologized over and over while he pulled cheesy pizza off the wall and offered to pay for the cleaning of the carpet, dry cleaning and damages to the wallpaper.

After almost an hour, Jonathan finally left the Hanson home. He knew it was too late to deliver the second order and the customer probably called to complain by now anyway. He walked back to the truck to find Billy sitting there, eating the pizza meant for his second delivery.

"Is the ambulance on the way?" asked Billy.

""No, the Hansons survived another day," replied Jonathan. They both just sat in the pickup for a while.

"You want a slice of pizza?" inquired Billy as he held up a cheesy piece. "It's really good."

Jonathan looked at Billy expressionless. He looked back, started the pickup and drove home, failing to finish his shift at the pizzeria for the evening.

The television went dim and the lights came back on in the studio. The two red faced candidates sat quietly on stage listening to the laughing and clapping of the audience. When things calmed down, Richard proceeded with the final portion of the election.

"Wow! What did I tell you, weren't those two segments great? Okay, now it's time to vote for your next class president. To vote for Margaret, dial CLASS MA (252 – 7762). To vote for Jonathan, dial CLASS JO (252-7756).

This time, the phones behind the audience didn't ring and Clearwater Cable didn't receive the usual wave of calls.

Dale leaned over and whispered to Joey, "Quick, go check the main telephone connection. I think we're having technical difficulties."

"No, we're not," replied Joey knowing exactly what was

happening. "We're experiencing temporary presidential candidate voting difficulties."

Jake looked around the pub from the bar and noticed the majority of his patrons started talking and ordering drinks. He turned to Janet and asked, "Hey, what gives? How come nobody's voting?"

"This show is great! I can't wait to get this idea back to the network," said Janet. She turned and whispered into Jakes ear, "People aren't voting because they don't believe in the candidates. You see, right now, these people are making a major statement by not voting."

"Huh?" replied Jake.

"Shhh, I'll explain it to you later tonight," said Janet with a smile and a wink.

"Oh, okay, tonight," said Jake as he understood Janet's subliminal suggestion.

At the recreation area, Simon observed the university students and noticed that they didn't seem interested in voting. They just laughed and talked amongst themselves.

"Mr. Weeks, what's happening," he asked.

"Just what I expected would happen, and the reason for my class project," replied Richard. "Did you notice what happened when everyone was given the opportunity to observe a candidate's performance and what happened when the candidate performed well? Observations were made, decisions were changed, and the majority voted with enthusiasm. People were able to make decisions based on clear-cut observations. Keep watching and see what happens when people are told to vote for candidates who they feel do not perform well."

Back at the television studio, Richard grinned like a Cheshire cat and then made an announcement. "Hey, I don't hear those telephones ringing. What's the matter, did you forget the numbers to call already? The audience began to murmur again and one guy shouted, "Get new candidates!" Another shouted, "These guys are lame!"

Richard held up one hand and his tone became serious as he said, "No, no everyone listen. When I said that these two individuals were the best candidates that qualified for the position of class president, I meant it. So, at this time, remember the other two candidates you voted for and think of all three individuals working together as a team. Judge their weaknesses and their strengths and then vote for your class president keeping in mind who will be assisting him or her as a team. Think about this one very carefully."

The phones began ringing slowly, both at the television studio and at Clearwater Cable. Voter's apathy was rearing its ugly head as students lost interest in voting. Some felt obligated to vote, while others refused because they didn't like the candidates for class president.

Richard looked into the television camera and said, "Keep those votes coming in. We're going to take a break and we'll be right back."

At the recreation area, Simon thought about what Richard had told him. Give people the opportunity to observe performance and they will vote enthusiastically if the candidate performs well. Take away that opportunity and make them choose from candidates they don't like, for whatever reasons, and they will hesitate or won't vote at all.

Why should the people have to vote for someone they don't like, thought Simon. They put the candidates in office at one time or another. Do people have the opportunity to directly choose a candidate for the presidential position, or are they given the opportunity to elect government officials who work their way up the political ladder. Simon was beginning to understand the reason for Richard's class project.

Simon's mind was flooding with observations. He went back in history to the time when America was untamed, underdeveloped, and unknown. To a time when someone was needed to explore, create, nurture and protect homestead land for a new civilization. A President at that time had to be a strong leader, trusted to do what was expected of him, and it was the responsibility of the people, Americans, to decide who that person should be. Americans were lean, mean, and hungry. They had power and passion, but they needed direction.

As decades turned into centuries, America grew and faced new and exciting challenges along the way. With each turn came a new direction and as our country grew, so did our government.

Our children and our land were our most valuable resources, and both needed to be maintained and nurtured for America to survive. Government agencies were developed to assist the people with education and farming. With the founding of each state came new political leaders. With each political leader came a new candidate for President. Department agencies turned into government branches. Our political system divided into the two party system which added more candidates for President. As time went by, our government had acquired bureaus, branches, departments and agencies as well as all the elected officials and employees to run it. The American government became extremely powerful and its sole purpose was to maintain our laws, keep us functioning as a democracy, and protect us from outside invaders. Eventually, it took on the responsibilities of the President.

Then came the Baby Boom and the population of America increased immensely. Americans were still being directed, but as our government grew stronger, the people, Americans were losing their power. They made comments that their votes and opinions didn't matter and they lost interest in voting. Some even stopped voting. As this went on, Americans lost their power and our government finally took control.

With the increase in population, our government experienced difficulty maintaining and keeping us functioning as a country. Americans relinquished their power and became overly dependent expecting the government to take care of them. Not to lead them, but to take care of them. Americans were no longer mean, lean or hungry and they had lost their power and passion.

Simon wondered if the President's only duty had become that of protector of our country and to keep outside invaders at bay. Did it matter who was President? Is anyone really leading our country like before? Are we still growing, just maintaining or worse, fighting a losing battle?

Simon gasped as he realized that his way of teaching and his ideas were not obsolete, they were stagnating. He had also become dependent on the government. Depending on it to tell him what to say in the classroom and how to teach, overriding his inspirational enthusiasm and innovative teaching style. He wondered what it was going to take to get America back on course, in the right direction, moving forward again.

Suddenly, Simon turned to Richard and smiled. He reached out and shook the young student's hand.

"Mr. Weeks, let's meet tomorrow and discuss your project. I'll meet with the Dean first thing in the morning just to make sure he's fine with what just happened. After that, it would be my pleasure to discuss your project. I'm looking forward to it."

Finally seeing a positive expression on the professor's face, Richard returned the smile and thanked him. They both turned and faced the television in time to see the end of the show.

Richard was on stage with all the candidates as he welcomed everyone back to the show. He looked into the camera and said, "For the next hour, we'll be taking votes for all positions. The results will be completed today and posted tomorrow at Boise State University. I'd like to thank our candidates for what they've done this afternoon. Everyone, please give them a big round of applause, if not for their performance as a candidate, then for their ability to entertain you."

The audience applauded with whistles and cheers.

Richard continued, "And a special thanks to all of you who participated in the voting process. This is Richard Weeks for *Class Campaign 2010* saying goodbye everyone!"

The show ended with Richard and the candidates waving goodbye as the audience applauded.

Chapter Seven
The Good News

Simon hadn't felt this good in years. He left the Dean's office feeling relieved and somewhat surprised. There was the expected lecture regarding university information being viewed on media or any kind, but to Simon's surprise, the Dean liked the show. He made a comment that old dogs can teach new tricks and he commended Simon on his ability to inspire his students with their class projects. He stated that this activity was a positive reflection of what the university can do in the eyes of the local community and he was very impressed with the overall involvement of the university students and faculty members. He told Simon to keep up the good work and continue his new style of teaching.

Simon couldn't wait to tell Richard. He entered his classroom and found Richard already waiting there.

"Oh, good morning Mr. Weeks, I've got good news,"

Richard was standing, briefcase in hand, with a big smile and he looked like he was going to burst.

"I bet it can't be better than my news, but you go first. How was your meeting with the Dean?" he asked.

Simon's tone became serious as he sat down at his desk and opened one of his books.

"Well, he was concerned that the project wasn't approved first," Simon looked up at Richard with a big smile and said, "but he loved it! He can't wait to see the results. I told him you'd have them ready and posted today. Are they available?"

Richard handed Simon a notebook containing his class project in detail as well as a video tape of the election.

"They're all here in this notebook. You'll find my project report and my theories on our current electoral system," said Richard.

Simon took the notebook and read the results. He peered over his glasses at Richard and said, "Just as you predicted. They voted with enthusiasm for the candidates they trusted and hesitated to vote for the candidates they didn't like. Who compiled your statistics?"

"Courtesy of Clearwater Cable," replied Richard, "now for my good news. A television producer called Clearwater Cable yesterday and said she saw my show. She liked it so much, she wants to meet with me tomorrow to discuss the possibility of putting it on national television. Professor, I'd like you to go with me."

"My goodness, why me?" asked Simon.

"Janet, Ms. Kendrick, wants to discuss my theories and why I created the show. I can give her my ideas and concepts, but I want someone who, um..."

Simon laughed and said, "You want an old dinosaur like me to be there in the event she asks the hard questions, right?"

"Well, I wouldn't have put it like that, but will you come? As far as I'm concerned, nobody else qualifies," replied Richard.

Simon looked at his schedule book, "National television huh, what time is the meeting?"

"Five o'clock," said Richard.

"I think I can make it. Where do we meet?" asked Simon.

"She said she'd pick us up at the university," said Richard. "I'm having my friend Joey from Clearwater Cable join us. If it weren't for him, there wouldn't have been a show. I'm not sure what she wants to know, just be ready for anything."

"Anything, well I'll do the best I can, and I'm going to let the Dean know about this," said Simon. "I'm sure he won't object. I'll tell him I'm going as a representative of the university and will fill him in on what's discussed."

"Great." Richard looked out the classroom window. "Professor, think about it. What if my project becomes a hit television show?"

Simon replied in a firm voice, "Let's not put the cart before the horse Mr. Weeks. Like you said, at this time, it's just a meeting and you don't even know what she wants to know."

Richard turned, looked at Simon, and then he looked at his watch.

"You're right, one step at a time. I've better get going or I'll be late for my next class," he said. "So, I'll see you in front of the university tomorrow at five o'clock?"

As Richard was walking toward the door, Simon waved goodbye and said, "I'll be there Mr. Weeks."

He sat at his desk and Simon thought about what just happened. The Dean is happy and likes this new style of teaching. A television producer was in town at the same time Richard had his election. Now, she wants to meet to discuss putting it on national television, possibly airing during an election year.

Simon started getting a funny feeling inside, but he wrote if off as his nerves acting up again. Deep down inside though, Simon's sixth sense was picking up on something. Things were happening for a reason, and this was just the beginning.

Chapter Eight
The Meeting

It was a brisk November afternoon. December was going to be brutal if this was a prelude of weather to come. The sky was dark with clouds and the newspapers predicted the possibility of snow. It was almost five o'clock and Richard, Joey and Simon stood in front of the university waiting for their ride. The temperature had to be below freezing as the three could prominently see their breath when they spoke. Their winter attire mirrored their personalities. Richard was dressed in a camel Burberry trench coat, brown leather gloves and a long beige wool scarf. Joey was dressed in a white and red, thick down filled Old Navy jacket, blue jeans and a red wool ski cap. Simon was dressed in a black and red wool sweater, charcoal dress pants and his favorite gray winter jacket he bought on sale at Sears. Suddenly, from around the corner came a white stretch limousine.

"Whoa, check it out," said Joey.

The limousine pulled up in front of the three and stopped. The driver lowered his window and said, "Good afternoon, are you the gentlemen who are to meet with Ms. Kendrick?"

"That would be us," replied Richard.

The driver got out and opened the rear door. Richard, Joey and Simon stood for a second looking at each other.

"Please get inside gentlemen. Ms. Kendrick is waiting," said the driver.

Richard was the first to enter the limo, then Joey. Simon looked around the campus as if he was looking for a witness. Hesitantly, he got into the limousine and they were on their way.

"You know what?" said Joey. "I've never been in a limo before. This is cool. Look at all the knobs and buttons." Joey started turning things on and off. He was acting like a kid in a candy store. One switch activated a small bar located in the center of the limousine.

"Like I said, this is cool," said Joey.

"Mr. Weeks, where are we going?" asked Simon.

"I don't know," replied Richard. "Ms. Kendrick told me to wait outside the university. I thought she was coming to pick us up."

Joey was inspecting the different items in the bar. While looking at the beer selection he said, "When she called the station looking for you, I thought it was a joke. I almost didn't give her your telephone number. What a mistake that would have been." He leaned over and whispered to Richard, "Is this stuff free or do we have to pay for it?"

Richard called out, "Excuse me driver, where are we going?"

"Don't worry gentlemen," replied the driver. "Sit back and enjoy the ride. Help yourself to anything in the bar."

"Wow, this is first class." Joey was reaching for a bottle of beer when Simon stopped him.

"Perhaps it would be a good idea not to have cocktails before our meeting," he said. "We should keep our heads clear until we get to where we're going."

"He's right Joey," said Richard. "We can always party on the way back."

"Just my luck," said Joey, "stuck in first class with a couple of party poopers. Okay, we'll do it your way."

After a few miles, the limousine began to slow down. The driver pulled over, stopped, got out and opened the rear door. Joey's eyes popped out as he watched the beautiful brunette get into the limousine.

"Wow, Richard. This really is first class," he said.

"Good afternoon, I'm Janet Kendrick. I know this is a bit unorthodox, but I'm on my way to the airport and this was the only time I could meet with you. I hope you don't mind." Everyone resituated themselves as Janet scooted into the seat. She and Simon sat in the back seat facing forward while Joey and Richard sat to the side. Richard reached out and shook Janet's hand.

"Hi Janet, I'm Richard. This is my political science professor, Simon Griswald and this is my friend Joey Sweet."

Janet shook everybody's hand, looked at Joey with a smile and said, "You're the one I spoke to at Clearwater Cable, right?"

"Uh huh," was all Joey could say. He was developing a crush on the executive producer.

"Like I was saying, I'm on my way back to California to meet with the network director of programming," said Janet. "Our network is looking for a new idea for a reality television show and I think your concept may be it. It's original and entertaining. I want to give a presentation the moment I get back, but I need some information. First, where did this idea come from?"

Richard looked at Joey and then at Simon. He knew if he told the truth, he'd be incriminating himself in front of Simon. How could he explain that his political science major was a charade, its only purpose merely to lead to a business career? He had to be very careful about what he was about to say.

"Well, being a political science major, I noticed some problems with our current electoral system and it's inadvertently affecting our country," started Richard.

"Inadvertently affecting our country? How?" asked Janet.

"Well, um," Richard was searching for the correct words.

Joey looked at his best friend and realized that he was heading into trouble. As friends do, he came to Richard's rescue.

"Richard's always telling me that the people need to get more excited about voting," interrupted Joey. "They need to get more involved with picking our leaders. He's always telling me that our government's way of doing things needs to change."

Richard looked at Joey and realized what he was doing. Joey had just returned the ball and now it was in Richard's court.

"That's right," said Richard. "Like I'm always telling Joey, our government is a magnificent ship, and like all great vessels, it needs direction. It's my opinion that our vessel currently lacks a captain." Richard looked over at Joey.

"That's right," said Joey. "According to Richard, our ship isn't moving. It's dead in the water, waiting for someone to take the helm. There are crew members on board protecting it, keeping other vessels from attacking, but it's not moving. It needs someone to lead it to uncharted waters, to a new location that will let us grow stronger, become more self sufficient and function better."

"Exactly," interrupted Richard. "Now, the question is which direction should we be heading and who should be captain? By all rights, the President should be leading our country in a direction where it eventually becomes self sufficient enough to take care of this country and then grow strong enough to assist other countries. If we can't take care of ourselves, how can we take care of others? At this point, I'm reminded of a saying my father always told me. You can't get fruit from a tree if the trunk is dieing."

Richard looked at Joey again.

"But, the President is too busy with terrorism and wars in other countries," continued Joey. "He's left the helm of our ship to protect the gates of our country. Perhaps that duty should be delegated to someone else allowing the President to focus on leading our country again."

"Right, that responsibility should be given to the Vice President," said Richard. "If the Vice President focuses his attention on protecting our country with the President's guidance, this will allow the President to…"

"Lead us in a new direction, where we grow stronger, become more self sufficient, and function more efficiently as a country that can assist others without jeopardizing our own stability," said Joey.

Janet and Simon sat in the back of the limousine, speechless for a moment, totally amazed at what they were hearing.

"I must say, that's the most interesting thing I've ever heard," said Janet, "but how does getting people more involved with voting fit into this concept?"

"The American people are the crew members of this magnificent ship," replied Richard. "They have to keep the lines of communication open with the leaders of our country, and the leaders have to listen to them. Just like in a business establishment, if the directors and executives don't listen to their employees and managers, they won't know what's going on in their own company. If they only react to what their competitors are doing, they may lead their company into bankruptcy. The people have to be given more power when it comes to deciding who leads this country and this country has to operate more like a business to become stronger. Our new leaders have to change our old ways of leading."

"In order to do that, our current electoral system has to change to give the people the ability to immediately elect who they see fit to run this country," said Joey. "Even if that means bypassing elected government officials who have been in office for years."

"Okay, I think I'm beginning to understand now," said Janet. "By allowing people to watch the candidates perform tasks on television, like you did, they can immediately decide who they want to run this country and vote accordingly. This makes the power of their vote stronger and more effective, right?"

"Right!" said Richard and Joey at the same time. They looked at each other, forgetting who was in charge of the conversation.

"Yes, but, this is just a television show, isn't it? I mean, we aren't talking about actually replacing the current electoral system with reality TV are we?" asked Simon.

"No, not at all," replied Janet, "I'm just collecting information for my presentation. I must say though, I'm very impressed. Professor Griswald, if this is an example of the students we have entering into the world, I have to say you're doing a fantastic job. As a matter of fact, may I be able to call on any of you if I need further research?"

"You can call on me anytime for anything," said Joey.

"You're so sweet," replied Janet, and then she laughed. "Oh, no pun intended. One more thing, may I keep the videotape of the show? I'd like it to be a part of the presentation."

"I guess it's okay, isn't it Professor?" asked Richard.

Simon thought about it for a second and then said, "Please do. I'll let the Dean know and if there are any problems, I'll let you know."

"Very good, here's my business card. Please feel free to contact me anytime." Janet looked out the window. "I didn't realize we'd driven so far. Our conversation was so stimulating that the time just flew by. We're entering the airport already. Straus, they did tell you which airline it is, I hope?"

"Yes they did Ms. Kendrick. We'll be there shortly," said the limousine driver.

"Straus will take you anywhere you need to go. Please help yourself to anything in the bar. Again, thank you very much for everything." Janet got out of the limo and waved goodbye. Straus closed the door and assisted taking her luggage to an already waiting skycap.

"I think I'm in love," said Joey as he watched her walk away.

Straus returned to the limousine and asked his three riding companions where their next destination would be. Not knowing how much longer the luxury ride would last, Joey popped open a bottle of champagne that was sitting in an ice bucket and handed Richard and Simon a couple of champagne glasses.

"Take us back to downtown Boise, Straus. We'll take it from there," said Richard.

"Very well," said Straus with a knowing smile.

Joey filled the elegant champagne glasses and suggested a toast be made. They lifted their glasses and clinked them in the air. Richard went first.

"Here's to a bright future filled with magnificent things to come."

Joey was next. "Here's to your new television show."

They both looked at Simon, who still had his glass in the air.

"Come on Professor, make a toast," said Joey.

Simon looked at Richard, then Joey, and said, "Here's to possibilities. Here's to a new television show that may create magnificent things to come. Here's to a country that gives us the opportunity to make possibilities become reality. Here's to America."

"Excellent," said Richard.

"Very good Professor," said Joey.

Afternoon turned into evening. Evening turned into night.

The limousine drove on to various destinations and the three men bonded. Simon was driven home. Richard and Joey were dropped off at their favorite hangout.

As the white limousine disappeared into the darkness, it began to snow.

Chapter Nine
The Grand Prize

Janet and Robert sat in the same overstuffed waiting room chairs they had four and a half weeks ago enjoying their cups of cappuccino the attentive secretary had brought them. This time, the chairs didn't seem so uncomfortable. They actually felt warm and cozy. Janet made her presentation to Frank Soars and now they were waiting for his response from the network brass. Robert leaned over and whispered to Janet.

"Thank goodness you came up with that wonderful idea. I told my wife not to worry, that you would think of something. She was threatening to call a divorce lawyer after I told her what happened to *The Gallery*. I hope they like it." He held tightly onto the briefcase containing a copy of their presentation.

"Don't' worry, I've got a good feeling about this," said Janet. "My gut instincts tell me they're going to like it."

The secretary picked up Robert's empty cappuccino cup and placed it on a tray and then said, "Ms. Kendrick, if you've finished with your cappuccino, Mr. Soars will see you now."

Janet nudged Robert's elbow and whispered, "See, we're getting the VIP treatment. That's a good sign."

The secretary opened the door to Frank Soars' office and Janet walked in as Robert trailed behind her. Frank was sitting at his desk, talking on the telephone, finishing his conversation with the corporate directors.

"Yes. I'll tell her. Of course, don't worry, I'll ask her. She just stepped in. Okay, goodbye." He hung up and greeted Janet and Robert.

"Janet, Robert, please have a seat."

He offered the two seats directly in front of his desk and like always, he pulled Janet's chair out and enjoyed the view as she sat down. Robert didn't wait for an offer. Frank returned to his seat, pulled out a cigar from his desk drawer and looked Janet straight in the eyes.

"You timing is perfect," he said. "I just got off the phone with the network brass. They reviewed your presentation and watched the videotape and they want me to tell you they enjoyed the pizzeria segment the most. Not only did they find the whole thing entertaining, but they thought the results for class president and the student's theories and observations were very interesting. They like the new idea and want you to get working on it as soon as possible. One question though, what's the grand prize? Whatever it is, they want it to be big and they'll assist in any way if you need help to make it happen. Do you have an idea yet?"

Janet looked surprised and said, "To tell you the truth Frank, I never thought about it. I was so focused on coming up with a new concept, I wasn't thinking that far in advance. The grand prize should be something politically related somehow."

"How about a position in the Whitehouse," Robert said quietly.

Janet and Frank both looked at Robert and waited for him to continue.

Nervously, he went on. "I mean, the corporate officers did say they wanted something big. Well, what could be bigger than a political position in the Whitehouse?"

"My God Janet, this man's a genius," said Frank. "No wonder you hired him as your assistant."

"Robert, that's a wonderful idea," exclaimed Janet. "Let's see, a position in the Whitehouse. One that's as close to the President as possible."

Janet pondered and remembered the conversation she had in the limousine with Richard and Joey. For the President to lead our country, the Vice President has to get more involved with security related issues.

"How about, an assistant position to the Vice President for six months or maybe one year?" suggested Janet.

Frank snapped his fingers, touched his nose and pointed at Janet.

"Perfect, I like that Kendrick magic. Okay, okay, hmmm." Frank began to frown.

"What's the matter Mr. Soars?" asked Robert.

"It's a good idea, but how do we create it?" asked Frank.

"Let's see, the corporate officers did say they wanted to help. Let's make them responsible for that project while we work on the show," said Robert.

"That's brilliant," said Frank. "It'll keep them busy, make them feel like a part of the show, and stop them from looking over our shoulders asking ridiculous questions. It's genius, pure genius."

"Good, we have a show, we have a grand prize, what's our timeline?" asked Janet.

"I was working on that when you presented your idea and I

realized it was a winner." Frank leaned back in his desk chair. "The timeline should go something like this. We have a basic concept, including contestants by February 2011. We begin advertising spring 2011. We start the show fall 2011 and it airs with the beginning of the 2012 Presidential Election. The timing is critical."

"Wow, you think we can do that?" asked Robert.

"If we want a hit show, we're going to have to," replied Frank. "The question is, do you think you two can do it?"

Janet and Robert looked at each other and then Janet smiled.

"Of course we can. With my magic and Robert's genius, we can do anything," she said.

"That's what I wanted to hear. You two get started and I'll give the guys upstairs a reason to earn their paychecks," said Frank.

Frank stood and shook hands with Janet and Robert. The meeting was over and everyone knew what they had to do. As they left the office, Robert stopped Janet in the waiting room.

"Ms. Kendrick, I just wanted to say thank you." Robert turned his head downward, looked at the floor and said, "There aren't too many people who believe in me. Just now, in there, it felt good to have someone...," he paused. "The things you and Mr. Soars said about me...," he paused again. Robert was having difficulty expressing what he wanted to say.

Janet sensed his difficulty. She reached out, took him by the hand and said, "Robert, look at me."

Robert looked up and replied, "I'm sorry, I'm not making any sense."

"Robert, listen to me," said Janet. "When I was looking for an assistant, you don't know how many people I interviewed. That time for me was very frustrating. Then, a polite and humble gentleman came into my office and presented a sincere and honest interview. I knew right then, I'd found my new assistant.

There was something genuine about this person and he possessed something deep inside that nobody else had. Right now, in that office, you proved me correct. For that, I want to thank you for letting me know I chose the right person to be my assistant."

Robert quietly replied, "Thank you Ms. Kendrick."

Janet patted him on the back as they headed out of the waiting room. She stopped when she came to the door and remembered four and a half weeks ago, it was Robert who was escorting her out of the room.

She turned to him and said, "You know Robert, I'm really looking forward to what you and I can do with this show. Now come on, we got a lot of work to do."

Chapter Ten
The Applications

The holidays were over and 2011 was underway. *The Gallery* had been taken off the air, and even though it was a bitter pill for Janet to swallow, she realized that in the television industry, one must survive the pitfalls and move on. She sat at her desk checking her email when she came across a memo from Frank Soars. She was half way through it when she called Robert to her office. No more than a few minutes later, he was standing in front of her desk. She continued to read and was talking to Robert at the same time.

"Mr. Soars just sent me a memo saying the corporate officers came through with their project," she said. "The position of assistant to the Vice President has been approved by the Whitehouse."

"That's great Ms. Kendrick. I was beginning to worry," said Robert.

"He also says they want to call the show *The Candidate Elect*. Well, I guess I can live with that," she said with a frown. "How are you doing with our list of contestants? The last time I checked we had a little over three hundred applications. Frank gave us the green light to start auditioning."

"Just a moment, I'll be right back," said Robert. He left her office and returned with a handcart loaded with four boxes of applications.

"Currently, we have one thousand, five hundred and twenty-seven applications. How are we going to narrow it down to only sixteen?" he asked.

"First, we begin weeding them out," replied Janet. "For the next two weeks, we go through each application and perform reference, credit, and background checks. We're looking for anything that may be construed questionable or inappropriate. These contestants have to be squeaky clean and when the list is condensed to only those who qualify, we begin the auditions."

"Who conducts the auditions?" asked Robert.

"Three people called panel members. They perform interviews similar to a talk show and it's all videotaped," replied Janet. "You know what? There is one person I'd like as a panel member. I met him on my way to the airport in Idaho. His name is Professor Simon Griswald. He teaches political science at Boise State University and the students he inspires are outstanding. I was thoroughly impressed with the conversation we had in the limousine about possibly changing our electoral system to benefit our country. Actually, it was one of his students who have me the idea for the show. Professor Griswald would make a perfect scholar panel member. Robert, could you see if he's available?'

"Certainly, any ideas about the other two?" asked Robert.

"Not at this time, but there's a few political types who owe me favors and I think it's time to collect. I'm sure I can convince a couple representatives from the Whitehouse to round out my panel," said Janet.

"Great, I'll call Professor Griswald," said Robert as he

rearranged the applications in the boxes. "That was Boise State University?"

"That's right, Simon Griswald. Professor of political science," said Janet.

Simon was somewhere on campus grounds when Robert called, so the university switchboard put him through to Simon's cell phone. Simon was walking back to his classroom when he heard his cell ring tone playing, *The Star Spangled Banner*.

"Hello," he answered.

"Hello. Is this Professor Simon Griswald?" asked Robert.

Unaware that this phone call was about to change his life from this point on, Simon innocently answered, "Yes it is."

"Professor, my name is Robert Garcia. I'm calling on behalf of Ms. Janet Kendrick. I believe you met her when she was vacationing in Idaho."

"Yes, I remember Ms. Kendrick. Does she need more information?" Simon's memories took him back to the limousine ride he enjoyed so much with Richard and Joey.

"Not exactly Professor. The reason I'm calling is to ask you if you would like to be one of three panel members to interview the contestants for our show," inquired Robert.

Not sure he heard correctly, Simon asked, "I'm sorry, what did you say?"

"Ms. Kendrick would like you to interview the contestants for the show. She was very impressed with you when she was in Idaho," said Robert. "She said you'd be perfect as a scholar panel member. Please say you'll do it Professor."

Simon almost dropped his phone. He had to sit down at his desk to continue the conversation.

"Me, a panel member, for the show?" he asked.

"That's right," replied Robert. "You were first on Ms.

Kendrick's list. We'll be doing interviews within the next two weeks. Do you think you'll be available?"

"I do have some vacation time coming, but this has to be approved by the Dean." Simon paused and then asked, "Are you sure she wants me?"

"Yes Professor, that I'm sure of. She specifically asked for you," said Robert. "I know you have to rearrange your schedule to make this happen, and I apologize for the short notice, but if you could get back to me within the next two days, that would be great."

Simon took the phone from his ear and looked at it, not knowing what to say. None of this was making any sense. For the longest time he doubted his teaching ability, and now, a producer for a television network is so impressed with him, that she specifically requests he interview contestants for her show.

For an instant, something came over him. Maybe the universe was telling him that he had been wrong to doubt himself and he was being given another chance to make a difference in the world. The purpose he yearned for could become reality in another way. This new feeling spurred on a new sense of confidence and he put the cell phone back to his ear.

"Okay, Mr. Garcia," he said. "I'll call you in two days. What's your telephone number?"

Robert gave Simon the number, thanked him for his time and hung up. Simon couldn't believe what just happened, but he called the Dean's secretary and made an appointment to discuss the possibility of taking time off for a trip to southern California.

Two days went by and Robert still hadn't heard from Simon. The network had processed three hundred and seventy-five applications and they were waiting for Janet to begin interviewing contestants. Due to the intense investigation process the contestants were put through, most of them had been disqualified for supplying false information, driving violations, questionable pornography purchases, drug related situations, poor health, obsessive gambling, tax fraud, possession of illegal weapons, alcoholism, racism, overwhelming debt, abusive behavior, identity theft, the inability to keep a job, shop lifting, and illegally spreading computer viruses. To be a contestant on this show meant you had to be virtually perfect. So far, they had only found twenty-three qualified contestants.

Robert was sitting quietly in the cafeteria looking over the reports of qualified contestants. All of a sudden, a look of astonishment enveloped his face. He jumped from his seat and bolted to Janet's office. He moved in such haste that when he reached her desk, he could hardly breathe.

"Yes Robert, what is it?" asked Janet.

"Robert tried to speak, but he couldn't catch his breath, so he pointed at the reports. Janet got him a glass of water and had him sit down.

"Now relax. What in the world has gotten into you?" she inquired.

It took a few seconds, but Robert did calm down enough to speak.

"Ms. Kendrick, we've been so focused on eliminating contestants that we forgot to look at the beneficial information about the contestants who qualified."

"What did you find?" asked Janet.

"Look at this page, see these four names?' Robert handed Janet the reports and she read the names out loud.

"Mr. John Alden, Mr. William Bradford, Ms. Priscilla Mullens, and Mr. Edward Winslow. I'm sorry Robert, what's so special about these four people?"

"According to the reports, these four people have the same names as those of the original pilgrims who came over on the

Mayflower and founded Plymouth Colony in 1620," said Robert. "Now, get ready for this. We're still checking on it, but there's a good chance that two of these contestants are blood relatives to the Plymouth Colony Pilgrims."

Janet stared at the reports and said, "You mean, the Mayflower before we had Thanksgiving, Mayflower? The Mayflower before America was America, Mayflower?"

"That's the one," answered Robert.

"When will we know which two people are related?" asked Janet.

"That's the problem," replied Robert. "I guess it's easy to pull up current information, but when we have to climb down a family tree, it takes some time to get to the roots. The information agency doesn't want to speculate or jump the gun, so this is all we have at this time."

"This information has to be confirmed and we don't have time to wait," said Janet. "It'll probably be quicker if we get the information through the interviewing process. That means we need to get our panel members together. Have you heard from Professor Griswald yet?"

"I'm waiting for his call. He's supposed to contact me today," replied Robert.

"Call him, and get him to come over here, and don't take no for an answer," said Janet. "Beg if you have to and tell him we'll pay for his flight here."

Janet walked to her desk and sat down. She kept looking at the four names on the report.

"I'm getting a funny feeling about this Robert, mixed feelings," she said. "They're not good or bad, just odd and it bothers me that I don't know what it is. I do know one thing though. We're going to need the Professor to sort things out."

She turned her attention from the reports to Robert and said, "If any of this is true, then we're sitting on a goldmine."

"Exactly," said Robert.

"I'm working on the Democratic and Republican panel members. We're drawing up their contracts right now and once they sign the papers, we'll put them to work. You go get the Professor here," said Janet.

"Certainly, Ms. Kendrick, anything else?" asked Robert.

"Let me know the moment you hear from him, and Robert..."

"Yes," replied Robert.

Janet smiled and said, "You are a genius."

"I'm beginning to believe that," said Robert with a smile.

Robert called the university and was surprised to learn that Simon had already taken vacation leave. While he was on the phone, he noticed the red message light was flashing on his display indicating he had a voicemail. He pressed the message button and was even more surprised to hear that it was a message from Simon. He was staying at a hotel in Los Angeles and wanted to set up a meeting.

"Perfect! He's here!" shouted Robert. He called the hotel where Simon was staying and was connected to his room.

"Hello," Simon answered.

"Professor!" exclaimed Robert.

"Mr. Garcia?" inquired Simon.

"Yes Professor, it's me Robert. Forgive me for sounding so excited, but I was surprised to hear you were in Los Angeles. Does this mean you'll be doing the interviews?"

"That's right. What do I need to do?" asked Simon.

"Stay right there," replied Robert. "We'll take care of your hotel bill and have a limousine bring you here. Have you eaten?"

"Only what they served on the plane," said Simon.

Robert laughed, "Oh no, we can do better than that. Tonight, you'll be dining with Ms. Kendrick at one of her favorite restaurants. You and she can discuss the details of the interviewing process. Our limousine should be there in about half an hour. The driver's name is Klaus."

"I know Klaus," said Simon. "He drove the limousine for us in Idaho. Great, I'll be waiting for him in the lobby."

"Wonderful. Professor, I'll let Ms. Kendrick know you're here and you'll be meeting with her in approximately an hour." Robert was thrilled that everything was falling into place.

After his conversation with Simon, Robert returned to Janet's office. He told her the good news and said he would call the restaurant and make reservations, but first, he needed to know how many people would be dining.

"Four," said Janet. "I'm assuming you'll be bringing your wife?"

"Me and Wauneta?" Robert asked with a double take.

"Of course, I'd love to meet Wauneta. Make the reservations for four people and dress semi-formal. I hope she can make it," said Janet.

Within two hours, Simon was meeting with Janet. They went over what he was to do as an interviewer and Janet had him sign the paperwork binding him to the deal. He understood this was going to take some time and he'd have to take a sabbatical from the university, but he was confident the Dean would support his decision.

Robert called Wauneta and told her they were going out for dinner. He wasn't surprised when she lost her temper because she didn't have anything decent to wear and she had already started dinner. After he apologized for being inconsiderate and thoughtless, she agreed to attend.

As she prepared for the evening, Janet couldn't shake that uneasy feeling about the Plymouth Colony contestants. Something wasn't right. She'd try to focus on something else, but her mind constantly wandered back to the contestants. What was it about these people? If they qualified, then what could be wrong? This was the first time in her life Janet wished she didn't have her perceptive talent. Then again, thought Janet, what kind of talent only gives you a feeling? A nagging, annoying, irritating feeling?

Chapter Eleven
The Plymouth Colony Contestants

February introduced the interviews and out of the fifteen hundred plus applications, only ninety-six had qualified, four of which had been labeled as the Plymouth Colony Contestants. Only a select few had made contact with them and those who had were instructed not to discuss them with anyone. Janet wanted to keep this treasure a secret. Frank Soars and the corporate officers didn't even know. Actually, today, Janet would be meeting them for the first time. She knew that to keep interest high, there had to be a hook, something unusual and interesting. She was going to start things off with a bang, and that's why these four contestants were scheduled to be the premier interviews.

On all days, this had to be the day she was running late. A traffic accident had caused a detour, making her drive out of her way to work, and if she hurried, she may make it in time to see the beginning of the interviews. She wanted to get there early and meet everyone and then go over the show agenda with Robert. Most of all, she wanted to know why she was still having uneasy feelings about the Plymouth Colony Contestants.

Janet stopped at a red light. She pulled out her cell phone and called Robert.

"Robert, this is Janet. Is everything set and ready to go?"

"Almost Ms. Kendrick, where are you?" asked Robert.

"Heading in the wrong direction, but I'm on my way in. What do you mean, almost?" asked Janet.

The light changed to green and Janet sped on her way. The battery in her cell phone was running low and the connection between she and Robert was fading in and out.

"The two p...bers didn't show up. The Professor's here...to know what he should do."

Janet realized that her panel members had cancelled at the last minute for some reason.

"Robert, tell Simon that he's going to have to do the interviews by himself. He'll be fine. Give him all the questions that the other panel members were to ask," said Janet.

"Ms. Kendrick...king up, but...think I understan...I'll tell the Prof...more thing, there's something...eed to know about today's contestants. Ms. Ken...hear me?" Robert's voice sounded urgent.

Janet started to get nervous. She knew something was wrong, and Robert knew what it was.

"What is it Robert? What about the contestants?" she asked.

Robert explanation was nothing but gibberish. Janet's cell phone battery was getting weaker and it interfered with the frequency as she drove further away from work.

"You nee...know that two...estants aren't...expect... Well,...of them...one... His...is...American...Ms. Ken...ear me?"

"Robert, I couldn't understand what you said. Robert?"

There was only silence now. Janet threw the phone onto the seat next to her and mumbled something halfhearted about technology. She stopped at another red light, looked into the sky and requested nothing else go wrong. As she expected, she made it to work just as the interviews were beginning. Robert stopped her before she entered the area where the show was being videotaped.

"Ms. Kendrick, I'm so glad you're finally here," said Robert. "Before you go in, let me fill you in on a few things. Two of the panel members were told that our subject matter was too controversial for their positions in the Whitehouse and they requested to cancel at the last minute. They found clever loopholes in our contracts that gave them the opportunity to do so. The professor agreed to do the interviews alone. He was a little nervous at first, but we managed to calm him down."

"Robert, what was it about the contestants? Did any of them cancel?" asked Janet.

"No, they all showed up," Robert said slowly. He had a peculiar expression on his face.

"What is it, tell me." Janet's tolerance was wearing thin.

"I think it's time you see for yourself." Robert motioned for Janet to follow him into the studio.

The show was being videotaped in front of a live studio audience consisting of about one hundred people. Janet could see that things were well underway and she saw Simon was already asking the contestant's career related questions. Then she looked at the contestants. She stood wide-eyed and said only one word.

"Oh."

Janet looked at the contestants for a while and then leaned over and whispered to Robert.

"So that explains that feeling I was having. Technically, nothing's wrong with these contestants, but a couple of them shouldn't be in front of that camera today." She quietly laughed,

"Robert, did I misunderstand something in school or were there Black and Latino pilgrims on the Mayflower?"

"That's what I was trying to tell you on the phone," whispered Robert. "Our reports showed why contestants were being disqualified, and nobody was disqualified because of his or her race. The agency is still following through with their family heritage investigations and the only thing we've received confirmed is that possibly two of the Plymouth Colony Contestants are blood related. Can you guess which two it may be?"

Of the four contestants on stage being interviewed, two men were Caucasian, one was Afro American and the woman was Hispanic.

Simon was doing quite well as host of the show and his timing was perfect. He asked the questions that were on the cards, waited for a response from the contestants, and gave the audience time to react. He made use of his college teaching wit when contestants started going on about themselves. He acknowledged what they had to say and then politely put them in their place. He was a natural.

First to be interviewed was John Alden.

Born in Washington D.C., in a middle class suburban home, John Alden received a masters Degree in Economics and was a self made man. He created and owned his own chain of luxury hotels and fine restaurants throughout the major cities of the United States. Currently, he was in the process of expanding to Europe. He knew what it was like to begin a business from scratch and felt that today's small businessmen were having a difficult time competing with power hungry corporate mega structures. His plan was to get into politics and keep the small businesses of America from becoming extinct. This would be his way of contributing to the next generation. He was thirty-six years old, six feet, two inches tall, weighed approximately two hundred and five pounds, had a deep rich voice, shaved his head and was Afro American.

Next to be interviewed was Priscilla Mullens.

Born in Phoenix Arizona and raised by her single mother, Priscilla Mullens received her degree in Communications. She went on to create and host her own evening local talk show called *PM*. She was known for speaking out, especially on political matters that pertained to the rights of Americans. After five years, she had achieved a large following, which showed in her ratings. Priscilla's talk show was doing so well, that it was on the verge of going national. She was thirty-two years old, five feet, ten inches tall, had long silky brown hair, beautiful brown eyes, a firm build and was Hispanic.

Next to be interviewed was William Bradford.

Born in Boston Massachusetts, into a family of nine children, William Bradford received his degree in Business Administration. In 1998, when he was only twenty-two years old, William created a trucking company that exported computers and computer equipment to Canada. He boasted a ten year marriage that included a son and daughter. From watching his children progress through public schools, William felt that America's educational system lacked in many areas and we were losing the ability to compete academically with our neighboring countries. At social gatherings, William always had something to say about the subject, usually ending with, "I know we have to protect our country, but someone has to be smart enough to build those bombs." William liked shopping at Sears and to relax, he did yard work. He was thirty-four years old, six feet tall, had a thick build from playing football in college and was Caucasian.

The last to be interviewed was Dr. Edward Winslow.

Born in Harrisburg Pennsylvania, into a well-to-do family, Dr.

Winslow went into the medical profession for political reasons. He became a General Practitioner in an attempt to create affordable medical care for the elderly. Edward expressed that he wasn't sure what direction America was heading and questioned political leaders and their ethics. He was married, had two sons and collected antique swords as a hobby. He exercised three times a week, and believed a healthy diet was the secret to a long life. He had brown eyes and brown hair, was thirty-five years old, was six feet, one inch tall, and was Caucasian.

Now that all the contestants had been introduced, Simon was directed to have the audience ask questions. He took a microphone to a rather sophisticated woman in the middle of the audience who raised her hand.

"Yes, what is your question and who is it for?" he asked the woman.

"Actually, Simon, my question is for you," said the woman with a smile.

Simon looked surprised and replied, "Me? My goodness, today must be my lucky day. Why yes, I am single at this time."

The audience laughed, as did the woman.

"Oh, I'm sorry, that wasn't your question. Please, what could you possibly want to ask me?"

"I'm from Massachusetts and I'm employed at the Pilgrim Hall Museum," said the woman. "It's very interesting that all the contestants today have the same names as some of the original pilgrims who came over on the Mayflower. Is there a reason for this?"

Edward and William looked at each other with a smile. John and Priscilla looked at each other and then at Edward and William.

"The cats out of the bag," said Janet.

"That was quick," said Robert.

Simon looked dumbfounded and then turned to the contestants and said, "You know, she's right. If my American History serves me correctly, all four of you do have the names of pilgrims. Are you members of a club or something?"

"Club?" inquired John.

"Pilgrims?" asked Priscilla.

"I think I know what's going on here," answered Edward. "William and I met before the show and found out we had something in common. We're descendants of the original pilgrims who settled this country."

"I know, what a small world," said William.

"I think someone thought all of us may have the same ancestry," said Edward as he looked at John and Priscilla who still looked confused.

"We don't belong to a club, but there are organizations that have members who claim to be related to the settlers of our country," said William. "Edward and I don't belong to any of these groups."

"Don't get us wrong, there's nothing wrong with these organizations and I'm sure that wonderful lady who asked the question may be affiliated with or knows someone who is a member," said Edward.

The woman smile and nodded.

"It's just, some members feel that, because of their bloodline, they're better than other people," continued Edward. "William and I keep our distance from that kind of thinking. We both agree that a healthy bloodline is important and we're proud of our pilgrim heritage, but we don't use it to belittle anyone."

"That's right, proud, but not smug," said William.

"We both feel that, what's most important about an individual as they go through life is what he or she contributes to society and to each other," said Edward.

The audience started clapping.

"That's very commendable," said Simon. His next question was directed at John and Priscilla, "Any comments?"

"I think we've been caught off guard," said John. "I had no idea who was going to be on the show today, nor did Ms. Mullens I presume."

"No, I didn't, and this is a hard act to follow," said Priscilla.

"Wait a minute, didn't John Alden and Priscilla Mullens get married on the Mayflower as it sailed to America?" asked Simon.

"Correct," said Edward.

"Hey, that's right," said William. Then he and Edward turned and smiled at John and Priscilla.

"Well then, perhaps there may be the sound of wedding bells again as we sail through this competition. John, Priscilla, any chance of history repeating itself?" asked Simon.

The audience giggled and laughed.

John and Priscilla looked at each other and if you looked close enough, you could see that John was blushing. Priscilla saw his embarrassment and came to his rescue.

"How could a woman refuse an invitation to dinner from the man who single handedly created an empire of luxury hotels and five star restaurants?" she asked.

John, seeing her kind gesture, utilized his charm and charisma to respond.

"How could a man fail to see the opportunity to ask such a beautiful woman to dinner and possibly dancing afterwards?" he replied.

This time it was Priscilla who blushed, which suggested the question of a possible romance between John and Priscilla.

The show went on and more audience members directed their questions to the contestants. There were some political related questions, but the audience seemed more interested in Edward and William's pilgrim heritage as well as the possible relationship between John and Priscilla. Later, something significant developed when the show was aired on television. The network received a flood of telephone calls and emails inquiring about the show and the contestants. Viewers insisted on being included in the question and answering process of the show. It was decided to include the television audience when approving which individuals should continue on as contestants.

This decision would later prove to be an essential communication device as well as an important means to measure ratings needed for the show.

Chapter Twelve
An Extreme Makeover

The Candidate Elect was drawing a lot of attention. You couldn't pick up a newspaper or magazine that didn't feature it somehow in an article or on the front cover. It was tagged as the world's first political reality TV show, and as the weeks went by, more and more people ordered tickets to be on the show. They continued to call and email their questions, comments and opinions about the contestants vying for the position of assistant to the Vice President. Their questions became more insistent and unyielding. People were actually taking the show very seriously. As time went by, possible contestants we're eliminating themselves from the list by committing suspicious acts as well as being eliminated by television and studio audiences. By April, 2011, the number of contestants for *The Candidate Elect* had been reduced to sixteen.

Simon Griswald was becoming a household name. Students who thought him dull and boring were now writing to him to congratulate him and give their support. With the show growing in popularity, the network corporate officers thought it was time to update Simon's look. Janet and Robert were instructed to create a TV special showing Simon getting an extreme makeover and they were on their way to his dressing room to give him the news.

"What do you think he's going to say" asked Robert.

"He doesn't have much choice," replied Janet. "In the beginning, as a panel member, his college professor look was fine, but with all the publicity the show is getting and the increase in ratings, he has to realize that his image is an essential part of *The Candidate Elect*."

"I don't think he understands. Remember when we told him we were moving him to a more secure residence due to his public popularity?" asked Robert. "Remember how he responded to that, or should I say, didn't respond?"

"I know. It takes some people longer to realize how important they're becoming, and in this industry, it happens so quickly," said Janet. "He still thinks he's just a professor of a university. Well, whether he likes it or not, he's about to become a star."

Simon opened his dressing room door and greeted Janet and Robert.

"Robert, Ms. Kendrick, how nice of you to visit," he said. "Please come in. Have there been changes in the show?"

"Not exactly with the show, as a matter of fact, we came to tell you some good news," replied Janet.

"That's right Professor," said Robert and Janet immediately gave him a stern look.

"Um, I mean Simon, Let's sit over here."

Robert took Simon by the arm and led him to the dressing room chairs. Janet sat next to him and Robert sat on the coffee table in front of both of them. Simon looked at Janet and then Robert waiting for one of them to begin talking. Thinking very carefully about what she was about to say, Janet finally initiated the conversation.

"Simon, would you say that *The Candidate Elect* has more to offer than just your average reality television show?" she asked.

"The number of people in the audience has grown immensely and I've been reading the articles and reviews. People actually like what we're doing. It's amazing how involved they've become," said Simon.

"Would you say we're creating a new standard for television as well as creating a new image for political leaders?' asked Janet.

"Well, I feel that *The Candidate Elect* utilizes television as a tool more than just a form of entertainment. It gives people an up close and personal look at their possible candidates. You rarely get to do that with our current political leaders," replied Simon.

"Exactly, now being the host of the show, what kind of image do you think you're sending to our viewers?" inquired Janet.

"Me?" asked Simon.

"That's right," Janet said with a smile.

Simon paused and then said, "I never thought about it. I mean, I never thought I had an image. There's a certain decorum we have to follow at the university, so I suppose they set the image."

"Exactly Simon, and like the university, we want to create an image for you as the host of *The Candidate Elect*. Right now, you still portray the image of a college professor," said Janet.

"How am I going to change my image?" inquired Simon.

Janet sat straight up in her chair and said, "That's the good news. The network wants to create a new image for Simon Griswald, the host. They want to give you a complete makeover and they want to air it as a television special."

"A television special?" Simon said nervously.

"Don't worry Profes...Simon." Robert was still having a difficult time separating Simon from his previous career title. "They don't do anything too drastic. They'll probably issue you a new wardrobe, perhaps a new style of eye glasses, color your hair and cut it differently, maybe even give you a tan."

"How would you like to go from sixty to forty?" asked Janet. "A little Botox here and there will get rid of those age revealing wrinkles. You'd lose twenty years in just a couple of hours."

"I don't know," Simon said apprehensively.

"A new image is a complicated thing," said Janet. "Why don't you think about it over night and we'll meet again tomorrow to discuss any concerns you may have." She held Simon's hand and said, "Simon, this is a good thing."

"I'll think about it," said Simon.

Janet and Robert said their goodbyes and left Simon's dressing room. Simon didn't know what to think. What did he know about creating an image? He never was a slave to fashion. The network could do anything they wanted to him and he wouldn't know if he looked better or worse, just uncomfortable. He needed advice. He needed someone he could trust. He needed someone who knew him and wouldn't let anyone make a fool out of him.

Simon picked up his phone and started dialing. The familiar voice on the other end answered with a cheerful hello.

"Hello, Mr. Weeks? This is Simon, Professor Griswald."

"Professor!" exclaimed Richard. "Hey everyone, it's the Professor. He's calling me on my phone right now." You could hear the sound of cheering in the background. "How're you doing Professor? You wouldn't believe how things have changed at the university."

"Mr. Weeks," Simon tried to interrupt, but Richard rambled on.

"Remember the three candidates elected as our student body leaders?" he said. "They got together with Clearwater Cable and created their own show. Each week, they have debates aimed at hot issued on campus. Topics are discussed pro and con and then put to a vote on television. The votes are tallied and the outcome is brought before the Dean for his review, and he either approves or denies them. It really works and there's been so much progress."

"Mr. Weeks," Simon tried again, but Richard went on.

"Speaking of Clearwater Cable, guess what? Joey was promoted to station manager. His boss was really impressed with the progress Joey's made for his business. They advertise your show all the time, and look at you, a big celebrity now. You know, if it weren't for my class project..."

"RICHARD!" Simon had to yell into the phone to get Richard's attention.

Richard stopped talking for a moment and then said, "I'm sorry Professor, what is it?"

"Mr. Weeks, I need your help," replied Simon.

"What's the matter?" asked Richard.

"They want to give me a makeover," said Simon.

"A what?" asked Richard.

"The network, they want to change my image and they're going to give me a makeover. They want to change me into someone else, and I don't know who that is." Simon sounded desperate.

"That's great Professor. What do you need from me?" asked Richard.

""You have a sense for fashion, you know me, and I trust you'll know what's best for my new image. Would you please come here and keep these people from making me look like an idiot?" asked Simon.

"Sure, you just way when and I'll be there. You can count on me," said Richard.

"Thank you Richard," Simon sounded relieved.

"Hey everyone, the Professor's getting a makeover and he

wants me to be his fashion consultant." The sounds of excitement could be heard in the background again.

Simon agreed to go through with the makeover and preparations commenced for the TV special. Richard flew to California and met with Simon. After catching up on past and current events, the topic of Simon's new image was placed on the table.

"So Professor," said Richard, "what is this new image you see for yourself?"

"I haven't a clue. I've gone through it over and over in my head, but all I see when I look in the mirror is me," replied Simon.

Richard sat and looked at the man sitting across from him for a moment and then said, "Do me a favor. Close your eyes and use your imagination."

"I've tried and it doesn't work," Simon said forlornly.

"Yes, but in the past you used your head. Now, you're going to use your mind. Come on Professor, I promise, this will work," said Richard.

Simon gave Richard a hopeless look and then closed his eyes.

"Take a deep breath and clear your mind of all thoughts." Simon did as Richard instructed.

"Now, see yourself just after you graduated college. You're at the crossroads of your life. Do you see it?" asked Richard.

Simon hesitated and then nodded his head yes.

"Look at where you are and what you're wearing. See everything around you." Richard was speaking very softly.

"Okay," said Simon.

"Tell me what you see," said Richard.

Simon started slowly, "There's a young man. He's wearing black stovepipe pants, a black suite jacket and a white shirt with a thin green tie."

"What year is it and where is he?" asked Richard.

"It's either 1968 or 1969," replied Simon. "He's standing outside on the sidewalk in front of a large window of a television store. The new color televisions have just arrived. There are a lot of people inside the store and they're watching the televisions."

"What are they watching?" asked Richard. His voice was still very soft.

Simon paused. His eyes were beginning to water and he attempted to hold back any tears that made an effort to escape.

"All the televisions are showing the same thing," he said. "It's a race riot. People are throwing and breaking things. Buildings are burning and the police are everywhere. People are being beaten, people of all colors. It's horrible. In the store, the people can't believe what they're watching. Some of them are turning away because they can see the redness of the blood in color now."

"Simon, what is the young man at the window thinking?" asked Richard.

A tear that Simon was holding back made its way out and ran down the side of his cheek.

"He can't believe how much anger and hostility there is and he wonders if it will ever end," he said. "What's happening to humanity? He doesn't understand why such a powerful nation would be at war with itself. He's looking at the people in the store watching the televisions. He can see the fear, the shock, and the disappointment in their faces."

"Go on Professor, what else is he thinking?" asked Richard.

"He's blaming everything on the assassination of President John F. Kennedy. He thinks that if he were still President, things would be different. A true leader wouldn't allow such chaos. A true leader would have created a more caring and peaceful nation."

The tear that ran down Simon's face was now joined by others.

"Professor, you can open your eyes now," said Richard.

Simon did so and wiped the tears from his face.

Richard patted Simon on the back and said, "Professor, you've just created your new image. Come on, we've got a lot of work ahead of us."

Chapter Thirteen
The President's Opinion

By the end of May, fourteen individuals were selected to be the main contestants for *The Candidate Elect* and the Pilgrim Colony Contestants were predicted to finish as the top four contenders. John Alden and Priscilla Mullens had their dinner together spurring on the suggestion of an alliance and possible secret romance.

Richard and Simon met with Janet and presented their idea for Simon's new image. Janet presented it to Frank Soars, who thought it was an excellent idea, and Simon's extreme makeover TV special was aired. His hair was cut, colored, and styled. His body was cleansed, oiled, massaged and tanned. Simon didn't want contact lenses, so his eyeglasses were replaced with a more modern pair that featured a chic frame and darkened in bright light. Most impressive was his wardrobe. A sixties style black Armani suite, white silk shirt with a yellow satin tie. What made his image powerful was the full-length black leather coat. The collar was raised behind his neck and the coat opened like a cape near his feet. In front of the bright studio lights, Simon's glasses tinted darkly enhancing his entire appearance. He looked like he just walked off the set of the movie *Matrix*, and he was hailed as the Political Terminator. His new image brought on a cocky smug attitude and his fans loved it.

The Candidate Elect was becoming one of the most popular television shows in America and the new American pastime was to participate in anything the political reality TV show could create. Whitehouse publicity consultants thought that this was a good opportunity for the President to secure his position with the people. Seizing an opportunity to jump on the bandwagon, they linked on to its political theme and applied the grand prize of assistant to the Vice President as if it were their contribution to America. However, the people were not stupid and they saw through this false claim. Through their comments, emails, and phone calls, people wanted to know exactly what the President's opinion was about the show. This created media mayhem, so much so, that the President eventually agreed to give a live press conference.

Frank Soars walked into Janet's office and dropped the morning newspaper on her desk.

"Did you see the headlines?" he rasped.

"Not yet," replied Janet. She picked up the newspaper and couldn't believe her eyes. On the front page, in big bold print, it read, "**WHICH CANDIDATE WILL HE ELECT?**"

"I don't believe it, he actually wants to give a press conference on *The Candidate Elect*?" she inquired.

"Why so surprised?" asked Frank. "It's only the most popular thing in America right now. The article says that the President will be making his comments tonight. The network brass will be watching it in the suite upstairs. They're hosting a little catered champagne celebration and they want you to be there."

Janet was still reading the paper while Frank spoke. She heard what he said and remembered that a few months ago, the brass was questioning her talent. Oh no, she wasn't about to pass up this invitation.

"May I invite a friend?" she asked.

"Of course, and bring Robert," replied Frank.

Janet laughed, "You read my mind. That's exactly who I was thinking about."

"One more thing, they want Simon to be there too. Could you invite him for me?" inquired Frank.

"It would be my pleasure," Janet said with a smile.

Robert and Simon agreed to attend the celebration and were requested to wear formal attire, as this was going to be an evening to remember. A presidential press conference aimed at a network television show would indubitably bring on more sponsors and viewers. You couldn't pay for publicity like this.

All eyes were on Janet as she walked into the suite wearing a dark blue evening gown accessorized with diamonds and sapphires. She was stunning. On each side of her, in black tuxedoes, were Robert and Simon. The three of them entered in grand fashion, like movie stars walking down the red carpet. Frank introduced Janet to each corporate officer and she made it a point to act charming and charismatic as she went from one established decision maker to another.

An announcement was made that the press conference was about to begin. A secret wall panel opened that revealed a sixty-two inch plasma television screen and as the light dimmed, everyone in the suite turned their attention to the television.

The President entered the room and made his way to the podium. After he was announced, the members of his audience, who consisted mostly of news anchors and writers for newspapers and magazines, began shouting, "Mr. President, Mr. President."

"Yes, down in the corner," the President pointed out to the crowd.

"Mr. President, who do you think is going to be the winner of *The Candidate Elect?*"

"I may be a bit premature, but my money is on Priscilla," replied the President.

"Mr. President, what are your thoughts about the show?" asked another reporter.

"I'm hoping that nobody has to eat any bugs," replied the President and everyone laughed.

"Seriously, Mr. President, with all the attention and overwhelming popularity of *The Candidate Elect*, what do you think the people are trying to tell you regarding our current political system?" came a voice from the crowd.

The President paused and thought about the question. He looked seriously out at the crowd.

"It is my feeling that *The Candidate Elect* is a harmless and fun way to get Americans somewhat involved in the voting process again. Over the last couple of presidential elections, there has been more and more voter apathy and perhaps, we may need to look at creating something more exciting that will make people want to vote again. Who knows, maybe this will stimulate a new concept for electing government officials."

All of a sudden, the audience went wild. They raised their hands and shouted out questions.

"Mr. President, are you saying our current electoral system is outdated and needs revising?"

"No, that's not what I," before he could finish, more questions bolted from the crowd.

"Mr. President, are you saying that the television and telephone will take the place of the voting booth?"

"Of course not, that's up surd," shouted the President.

"Mr. President, due to the popularity of the show, are the people of America saying that they're tired of waiting and are taking things into their own hands by creating their own revised voting system?"

The questions started coming all at once, not being heard or understood by anyone. This wasn't what the President was expecting and he and his delegates stood, shocked at how the conference had turned to chaos. This made the President feel very uncomfortable and he raised his arms to get everyone's attention.

"People, people, please," he shouted and the crowd quieted down.

"Remember where you are and behave in a civil manner. First, let me apologize for my comment earlier about this show becoming a source for changing the way we vote. That's not what I meant. I guess I didn't take the question seriously, and again, I apologize for that. Let me assure you that *The Candidate Elect* is only a television show, nothing more. Our current voting process has been in effect for hundreds of years and will not be replaced. The electoral system is what made this country what it is today. Now, at this time, I have other matters that need my attention. Thank you for your time."

The President was leaving the conference room, but the questions kept coming.

"Mr. President, what is the current condition of our country?"

That question fell to deaf ears as the President was being escorted out of the conference room.

Back at the network suite, the plasma television went dark and regained its position behind the wall. The lights were brightened and everyone started clapping. The corporate officers began talking amongst each other, some even slapping their hands together in the air, high-five style.

"Great! Absolutely great," shouted one of the officers..
"Better than expected, much better," shouted another.
"Why do we need an advertising committee when we have Ms. Kendrick?" asked another.
"Here, here everyone, a toast to Janet Kendrick." One officer lifted his glass of champagne and the rest did the same. Frank took a drink from his glass and looked at Janet.
"So, Ms. Kendrick, what's our next move?" he asked.
Janet took a sip of champagne, smiled and said, "I think it's time we find out if the President is right. We have some time to fill before we begin the competition. Let's see if Americans are really happy with their current electoral system."

Chapter Fourteen
The Poster

The network created a poster for the show. It displayed Simon as the Political Terminator, standing in full costume, facing forward with a cold sunglass stare. His legs were spread, standing on a big screen television, one hand on his hip and the other pointing directly at the person viewing the poster. In the background were blurry smudges of black and red with the obscure materialization of smoke from burning voting booths. Above his head read the caption, *"Speak And Be Heard."* Below him, on the television screen, showed the title of the poster, *"The American Voting System Poll."*

People were being asked their opinion. Did they like the current voting system that's been around for hundreds of years or did they think a new system should be created? Advertisements were aired on television as well as the internet. The posters were placed in strategic locations around Los Angeles as well as being available for sale throughout America. The network would run the poll until the end of June and would have the results announced on the Fourth of July.

Whitehouse representatives didn't look positively on what the network was doing, and they made a request to call the poll off. As expected, the request was denied. News of what was happening leaked out to the media and it was being publicized in every way. This was good advertising for the show, and it kept the government from pulling any unnecessary punches. Then again, knowing that the United States government usually gets what it wants, the corporate officers stayed alert.

Back at Boise, Richard and Joey were enjoying their summer vacations. Richard was between semesters and Joey had taken two weeks off from Clearwater Cable. The two were in the midst of the Pacific Northwest wilderness enjoying a hiking excursion to get away from it all. Fresh air, sparkling streams and tall timber embraced them as they hiked the winding trails. Richard felt that this was a good time to talk to his best friend about a secret he'd been keeping since his return from California.

"So, Joey, how many Political Terminator posters do you have hanging on the walls at Clearwater Cable?" he asked.

"They've become our new wallpaper," laughed Joey.

"Get this, my parents bought one. They think this is the beginning of something big," said Richard.

"My parents don't have a clue," said Joey. He was climbing over a large tree that had fallen over the trail.

"Joey?" inquired Richard.

"Yea, what is it?" Joey was spread eagle on the log. His jeans had snagged on the bark and he was trying to get loose.

"What do you think about the poll? I mean, do you think we can or will change the way we vote in America?" asked Richard.

Joey talked as he worked his jeans from the bark. "Well, as for changing things, it's going to take something big to make that happen. You have to admit, this system has been around for a long time, and it was good in the beginning."

Joey stopped what he was doing and looked at Richard.

"In the beginning, it was a good system," he said. "Does that mean it is now? I don't know Richard. Some things seem to change quickly, like fashion and technology. Others seem to change slowly, like religion and politics. It would be nice if religious beliefs and political ideas progressed as quickly as everything else, but that doesn't seem to be happening."

"I know," said Richard. "It feels like we're falling out of sync with the world and each other. Poverty, pollution, global warming, extreme weather, wars around the world and now terrorism, as we keep fighting to stay separate, it just keeps getting worse. Maybe we've hit the point where it's not all about ownership of power and money. Perhaps we're supposed to be learning to live with each other as one being on this planet."

"You mean, like human beings?" asked Joey.

"Yeah, like human beings," replied Richard.

"So, the question is, will a simple change in how we vote place us on the road to becoming harmonious human beings?" asked Joey.

"A change in leadership could do that," replied Richard. "There has to be a way to give people more power to elect leaders who can make positive changes. If people don't believe that the candidates waiting to be elected, then why should they vote? They have to have better access to selecting and electing their own candidates, especially when the status quo political candidates aren't listening to them."

"If they can't do the job, they should be terminated by the Political Terminator. Isn't that his job?" laughed Joey.

"Hey, don't make fun of the Political Terminator. That image took Simon and me a long time to create. Which brings me to the subject I really want to talk about," said Richard.

"And what would that be?" asked Joey, finally freeing himself from the tree bark.

"When I was with Simon in California, he asked me a question. I couldn't give him an answer at that time because I was still in school. It's summer break now and I have to give him an answer," said Richard.

"What's the question?" asked Joey.

"Simon asked me to move to California and be his manager until the end of the show. I know it sounds crazy, but he feels all alone, and for some reason, the old guy likes me," said Richard. "He likes the way we work together and he trusts me."

"Richard Weeks, manager of the Political Terminator. Yup, it does sound crazy, but it sounds like the Professor needs you," said Joey. "If you're asking for my opinion, I say go help him out. You'll make a great manager. One thing though, what do your parents say?"

"Like I said, they bought the poster. They think it would be to my advantage to network in the Hollywood social scene and create some connections for my future lobbyist career," said Richard.

"You, a lobbyist, now that's really crazy," said Joey.

They walked for a while without talking, then Richard made an observation.

"It's funny, you still call him Professor, but to me, he's Simon. I guess it's because of his new image," he said.

"He'll always be the Professor to me," said Joey and then he paused. A little while later he said, "So, I guess I won't be seeing you next semester. You'll be in California."

"That's right, and don't think this lets you out of any best friend obligations. If I ever need a favor, I expect you to be there," said Richard.

"What would the manager of the Political Terminator need from the station manager of Clearwater Cable?" asked Joey.

The two young colleges continued forward on the rocky trail. Richard patted Joey on the back and replied, "You never know Joey. You never know."

Chapter Fifteen
The Kimberly Cross Show

Kimberly walked briskly to the arena. Her wardrobe designer followed, adjusting the stylish black blazer Kimberly wore to ensure it would give off the proper effect when the spotlights hit it. The show coordinator was at the arena entrance waiting to go over the show's agenda, but Kimberly had no time for that. She'd been promoting today's event for weeks and the day had finally come for her to talk to the Political Terminator and the Pilgrim Colony Contestants. She ran past the coordinator and burst into the filming arena with her hands in the air. The television cameras zoomed in on her and the audience went wild. Her wardrobe designer breathed a sigh of relief as the spotlights beamed down on Kimberly's black blazer, causing the sequins to sparkle and glisten like colorful fireworks exploding in the night sky. Kimberly energetically greeted her audience and thanked them for being there, but they continued to clap and scream with excitement. She placed a finger to her lips in an effort to quiet them down, and they responded.

"Wow! What a great audience," she exclaimed. "You guys are

fantastic! Who out there hasn't heard of that wonderful political reality television show, *The Candidate Elect?*"

Her audience replied by clapping and shouting.

"That's what I thought. Guess who's here today?" she asked.

Kimberly stood with her legs apart, one hand on her hip and the other pointing at her audience.

"We've got the Political Terminator and the Pilgrim Colony Contestants!" she shouted and her audience responded with enthusiasm.

"We also have the producers from the reality TV shows, *Staying Alive*, *The Rookie*, and *The Crooning Icon*, to give us their views on political reality TV," advised Kimberly. "Then we're going to take a sneak peek at today's statistics for *The American Voting System Poll*. So, sit back and relax, because we're going to do all that, right after this."

The show went to commercials.

The show returned with Kimberly sitting in a plush armchair designed to fit the theme of the show. In a line at an angle, next to her, were five similar chairs, their colors being red, white and blue. Kimberly's armchair contained all three colors with stars and stripes. In the background was an enormous floor to ceiling copy of the Political Terminator poster. Kimberly welcomed everyone back to the show and introduced Simon, John, Priscilla, Edward and William. They all walked to the arena, greeted Kimberly and took their seats. Simon sat next to Kimberly and stared at this poster. He'd never seen himself on such a large scale. Kimberly leaned over to him.

"Does he look familiar?" she asked.

"My God!" shouted Simon. "Who is that handsome, dashing man?"

The audience laughed, setting the stage for Kimberly to begin he interview.

"Simon, I was told that you're a professor at Boise State University and this show originated from a class project organized by one of your students. Is this true?" she asked.

"As a matter of fact, that is true," replied Simon.

"How does a class project become the most popular reality television show in America?" asked Kimberly.

Simon thought about her question for a moment.

"It just happened," he said. "The class project was an experimental class election. When the election was aired, Janet Kendrick, the executive producer of *The Candidate Elect*, saw it and thought it would be a good idea for a reality television show. She presented the idea to her network and the rest is history."

"What happened to the student who created the class project?" asked Kimberly.

"Believe it or not, he became my manager," laughed Simon. "His name is Richard Weeks and I'd like to thank him, because none of this would have happened if it weren't for him."

Simon clapped and the audience did the same.

"Are you going to go back to being a professor or is being a political terminator your new profession?" inquired Kimberly.

Simon paused, turned and looked at his poster. Then he turned back and looked at Kimberly.

"You know, all I ever wanted was to be a part of creating a future President of the United States," he said. "For some reason I thought that becoming a political science professor would give me the opportunity to do that. I've been teaching for many years now and that hasn't happened. I don't know. Maybe assistant to the Vice President is as close as I'm going to get."

Kimberly leaned over, close to Simon and said, "Simon, never say never." She leaned back in her seat and looked at the contestants. "You just might find the next President of the United States sitting somewhere in one of those seats."

"Hi John and Priscilla, anymore dinner dates lately? So what's up with that?" she asked and her audience started laughing.

"Hi Kim," replied John. "Yes, Priscilla and I have been seeing more of each other."

"But, that's all going to end when the competition begins in the fall," said Priscilla.

John turned, looked at Priscilla and inquired, "It will?"

Priscilla sat and looked at John, and then Kimberly took over.

"John, you don't seriously believe that you and Priscilla will continue to have a relationship while competing for the same Whitehouse position?" she asked.

"Why not, why can't we work together as a team, both supporting each other along the way?" he replied. "The only time Priscilla and I will be competing against each other is when we're placed on separate teams or at the end when it's just Priscilla and me."

John turned and looked at Priscilla and said, "And I know we're going to make it to the end together."

John's heartfelt comment touched the audience. Priscilla sat, looking at John. She was caught off guard, not realizing that their sociable relationship had meant so much to him.

'Priscilla, how do you feel about that?" asked Kimberly.

"I'm speechless," replied Priscilla. "I'm sorry John, I just assumed that things would change when the competition begins. I had no idea you felt this way, but now that I know, I think working together would be a wonderful idea."

Kimberly turned to Edward and William.

"Where does that leave you two? Are you going to form your own alliance as well?' she asked.

Edward and William looked at each other with a smile.

"Not exactly," said Edward. "William and I were hoping something like this would happen and we're behind them all the way."

"That's right," said William.

"I don't understand," replied Kimberly.

"Remember, we're descendants of the original pilgrims. If you look at what's happening, it's almost as if history is repeating itself," said Edward.

"It's a sign. Think about it," said William. "Just like the original pilgrims on the Mayflower, we're on a voyage too. Only, our journey isn't to a new country, instead, this trip is to the Whitehouse. Also notice as we go through our trials and tribulations, something wonderful is happening. A romance is forming, a similar romance that occurred on the Mayflower back in 1620."

"John and Priscilla didn't know each other until they met on the show, and look how far things have progressed between the two of them," said Edward. "William and I are going to do everything we can to nurture this relationship. Deep down inside, we feel that this is all happening for a reason. It could be an indication that we've been given a second chance to do things differently. In a way, history is repeating itself."

Priscilla and John sat looking at Edward and William with the same surprised expression as Kimberly.

"So, are you saying you aren't going to be competing for the Whitehouse position?" inquired Kimberly.

"Of course we are. We're all going to do our best to make it to the Whitehouse," said Edward. "As John and Priscilla join forces, William and I will join forces to ensure this voyage to the Whitehouse is a smooth one."

Kimberly leaned over to Simon and said, "How many contestants are there?"

"Fourteen," replied Simon.

"This is the most interesting competition I've ever seen. History, romance and support all rolled up in four contestants," said Kimberly. "Simon, I want you to come back with some of the other contestants so they can give us their viewpoints and what they have planned. Would you do that for me?"

"Sure," said Simon.

"I wish we could talk more, but we must say goodbye. I'm so glad we had this opportunity to talk with all of you today. John, Priscilla, Edward, William, good luck," said Kimberly.

Everyone thanked Kimberly and waved goodbye to the audience as they left the arena and then the show went to commercials. When the show returned, Kimberly introduced the producers. There was Christopher Cohen, executive producer of *Staying Alive*, John Harrison, executive producer of *The Rookie*, and Trevor Adams, director and executive producer of *The Crooning Icon*. Once introduced, Kimberly started with her interview.

"If I understand correctly, *The Candidate Elect* is a reality TV show about politics. What on earth are these contestants going to do? What kind of tasks can they perform to become assistant to the Vice President?" asked Kimberly.

"First of all, I think it was a brilliant move to include the television audience as much as they did during the interviewing portion of the show," said Trevor.

"I agree," said Christopher. "That allowed the public to get to know the contestant's personal background in advance, instead of during the competition. This way, the rest of the show can be entirely designed for performance."

"Performance, what kind of performance?" asked Kimberly

"I suppose it depends on the requirements of the position," said John.

"They should be given physical and mental challenges so we can see how strong they are. Working in the Whitehouse is not meant for the weak," said Christopher.

"If it were my show, I'd take them out of their safety zones and put them in situations that make them completely uncomfortable," said Trevor.

"Why would you do that?" asked Kimberly.

"As a political leader, you can't pick and choose the easy tasks on a daily basis," said Trevor. "There are times you have to deal with extremely stressful conditions. Situations that may involve a phobia you haven't conquered or a traumatic event in your life that hasn't reached closure. These conditions can affect a person's decision making process. If they can't handle the situation, they shouldn't be in that position."

"Wow, that sounds kind of cruel, but you're right. You're absolutely right, and here I was thinking that they should know something about different cultures," said Kimberly.

"That's a good point, and it can easily become a task in this type of show," said John.

"So, if I understand correctly, what you're telling everyone is the tasks should be demanding, complex, and multifaceted, just as long as they relate to the position," said Kimberly.

"Yes, and they should continue to keep their audience involved. Maybe even have them create some of the tasks for the show. That would keep them interested and give them a sense of ownership," said John.

"That's an excellent idea," said Trevor. "Have the television audience send in their ideas for performance tasks and find out what Americans think political leaders should be held accountable for. The audience members who have their tasks applied to the show win a prize."

The audience liked the sound of that and started clapping.

"I hope Simon is listening to this. Simon, are you still here?" Kimberly looked behind her pretending to look for Simon, and then she turned back to the producers.

"Before we go to commercial, there's one more question I'd like to ask," said Kimberly. "Seeing how Americans get involved with voting when it comes to reality television, if it were designed properly, can reality TV be used as a means to elect our political leaders?"

The three producers looked at each other, hesitant to give their opinions.

"Did I go someplace I wasn't supposed to?" asked Kimberly.

"Yes and no," answered Christopher. "You have to understand how ridiculous that question may sound, but it really deserves a thoughtful answer. America is a country where anything can become reality. In the 1950's, Hollywood showed us flying around in outer space. In the 1960's, we turned that into reality by landing on the moon. When it first started, reality television was a modern version of the old television game shows. You had contestants performing an act for a prize. In *The Candidate Elect*, you have a contestant performing a task for a position in the Whitehouse. It takes the same concept, and applies it to something more meaningful."

"I agree," said John. "*The Candidate Elect* is a link that's taking us from performing reality television to performance reality television."

"Job performance is what it's all about, and a position in the Whitehouse is a career," said Trevor. "I guess you could compare the President and Vice President of the United States to a CEO and COO of a large corporation. In both situations, someone has to make a lot of important decisions to keep the company or country going."

"A political candidate should be treated like a person being considered for a high salaried position of a large corporation," said Christopher. "This individual should have to go through an interviewing process and probationary period. This is what *The Candidate Elect* is presenting to us."

"It's funny, and what I'm about to say may get me into trouble, but if a corporation operated the way our government runs our country, it would go bankrupt within six months," said John.

"Why is that?" asked Kimberly.

"Cutbacks in our educational system are similar to lack of training in a business," replied John. "Bills, amendments, and courtroom hearings that take months to years for a decision are all similar to poor communication and decision making skills in a business. Reducing or completely eliminating Social Security is like a long term employee losing his company pension. Now, the big one is our national debt. This is comparable to a staggering company overhead and that alone will put any CEO in the poorhouse, especially if it persists for a number of years."

That comment was the clincher, and the audience responded with shouts, clapping and whistles.

"What you're saying is that our country would operate better if run like a large corporation, and reality television can be the link that takes us from what we have now to something more productive?" asked Kimberly.

Right after she asked her question, she remembered what Edward and William said about John and Priscilla's romance being a sign giving us a second chance to do things differently, and it made her feel a little uneasy.

The three producers agreed and the audience started clapping.

"Let me add on more thing," said Christopher. "When receiving information, people use their senses, and the three most important are visual, auditory, and kinetic, which means performing the action. You commented on how much more people enjoy voting during a reality television situation compared to a real political election. If you noticed during an actual political election, candidates send us information two way, visually and auditory. We read their campaign information and see them on television or during public rallies. During debates or political speeches, we hear what they have to say. That satisfies only two of our three information senses. During reality television, contestants send information visually, auditory and kinetically. We actually see them dance, juggle, or eat fire. We hear them sing, play an instrument or read a poem. The whole time, they're performing an action and that action is the most important, because it justifies the first two senses, thus satisfying all our information senses. Once all senses have been satisfied, we are eager to vote. Now, can this be applied to an actual political election? I guess we're about to find out."

Kimberly wanted to continue her conversation with the producers, but she knew her time was limited and she had to go to commercials.

"You can't imagine how enlightening this show has been, and I wish we could keep talking, but I must say goodbye," she said. "Thank you all for being on the show today."

Kimberly shook hands with the three producers and the show went to commercials. When the show returned, Kimberly was alone in the arena. Behind her was a large electronic tally board decorated with brightly colored red, white and blue lights, streamers and American flags. On top was a banner that read, *The American Voting System Poll*. In the center were two digital panels. One was labeled, "Make a new system" and the other was labeled, "Keep the old system." She welcomed everyone back and went on to explain the final segment of the show.

"It's just about time for us to take a sneak peek at today's numbers for *The American Voting System Poll*," announced Kimberly.

Off to the side, the show coordinator was waving frantically to get Kimberly's attention. She saw him waving and stopped what she was doing. He started whispering something, but she couldn't hear him.

"What? I can't hear…" She turned and faced the audience. "Excuse me for one moment. I have to attend a short meeting with my show coordinator."

Kimberly strolled over to where he was and listened to what he had to say. Her face lit up and then she quickly returned to her original spot in the arena.

"You aren't going to believe this. I was just informed that because of today's show, the poll had an overwhelming amount of votes," she announced. "The statistics have been altered by eight percentage points, which has evidently made a big difference in the poll."

Kimberly paused, looked at the tally board and then said, "How exciting, my show made a difference in a national poll. This is better than the day I gave away a neighborhood of homes to fifty people in the audience."

She turned, pointed to the tally board and shouted, "Show us the numbers!"

The digital panels flashed random numbers and after about ten seconds the numbers were revealed. Kimberly stood and stared in amazement at the board as her audience went wild. Prior to the show, the poll statistics were at a 50% - 50% stalemate, and because of her show, the tie had been broken. The percentages were now 58% for creating a new system and 42% for keeping the old system. Kimberly turned toward the television cameras with the large digital displays illuminating brightly behind her and then she started laughing.

"I guess I did it again, another television first. Come on America, keep those votes coming in!" she shouted.

The show reached its conclusion and Kimberly thanked all her guests for being on the show. She said goodbye to her audience and headed toward the arena exit. As the audience clapped and the theme music played, Kimberly took a moment to look at the tally board one more time and in her mind, she played back the events that had taken place on her show. She waved goodbye to her audience for a final time and left the arena. Staff and crew members patted her on the back and congratulated her as she headed for her dressing room. Once inside, Kimberly closed the door, walked over to her mirror and looked at her reflection.

"Damn KC, what just happened?" she asked herself.

Chapter Sixteen
The Whitehouse Reacts

Fireworks took precedence in July. The twilight displays were praiseworthy, but the flare up that took place at the Whitehouse was much more spectacular. The network's excessive promoting of *The Candidate Elect*, the President's press conference and *The Kimberly Cross Show* all had an impact on Americans and it showed in *The American Voting System Poll*. On the 4th of July, the network announced the final statistics which were 71% for creating a new system and 29% for keeping the old system. Close to one hundred and twenty-two million Americans made it clear that they wanted a new system for electing their political leaders. Whitehouse staff thought it would be a good idea to make some kind of comment on the situation, but the President didn't feel the situation was that important and declined a request for another press conference. He looked at the poll as a mere Hollywood promotion to sell a television show, however, it was creating a wrinkle in his political plans. Therefore, he handled the situation in his own way. He withdrew the position of assistant to the Vice President from *The Candidate Elect* and made a discreet, but firm comment that if the network continued with their promotions, their FCC licenses would be up for serious review, which would shut the show down for at least months. With that understood and the position withdrawn from the show, the President thought he had sufficiently handled the situation.

The network corporate officers were in a dilemma. If they continued with the show, they would have the wrath of the Whitehouse upon them. If they cancelled the show, they would have the wrath of their viewing audiences upon them. To make matters worse, their ratings were skyrocketing through the roof, breaking all previous network records, and sponsors were still lining up outside their door waiting to be a part of the new political reality television experience.

Frank Soars knew there was a solution to this problem. They couldn't let the concept die, but they could cancel the show. It was decided that *The Candidate Elect* would be taken off the air, and another political reality television show would be created that didn't need any assistance from the Whitehouse.

Chapter Seventeen
Millenica

"Let me guess, we lost the position to the Whitehouse?" asked Janet as Frank entered her office. She knew he had just met with the corporate officers.

"Better than that, we were told to cancel the show or our FCC licenses would be up for review, which could shut us down for a couple months," he replied.

"So, the Whitehouse is stooping to blackmail. Good, that means they know we mean business. What's the brass want to do?" asked Janet.

"Kill *The Candidate Elect* and create a clone with a different name that can operate on its own. How do you feel about that?" asked Frank.

Janet sat for a while and thought about his question. Frank knew she would come up with a good idea. He was just giving her time.

"Maybe they're right," she said. *The Candidate Elect* got us to this point, but we've always needed approval from the Whitehouse to make it work. They had us under their thumb for a while and they think they still do."

Janet walked over to the window and looked at the people below on the sidewalks and city streets. She paused for a while and then turned and looked at Frank.

"We don't need the Whitehouse anymore Frank, and do you know why?" she asked. "Because we have the people behind us, we've created our own political power. It's all starting to make sense. From the moment they started calling and emailing their comments about the contestants. They've been talking to us this whole time, pleading to be heard. That's why the show is so popular. We've got to give them what they want Frank. If we don't someone else will. Let's build another show that focuses on giving Americans what they want. Let's give America a new system for electing political leaders."

"Political power from the people, you say? So that's why the Whitehouse feels threatened. Okay, keep going, I'm listening," said Frank.

Janet started pacing back and forth as she spoke out loud.

"What can we do? What do we have? Politically, what's available to us to make this happen?" she asked.

All of a sudden, she stopped pacing and snapped her fingers.

"Of course, it's been sitting there right in front of us this whole time. Why didn't I think of this sooner?" she shouted.

"What?" shouted Frank.

"That political party that's neither Republican nor Democrat, that beautiful, wonderful, Independent Party system," she said and she danced over to Frank and kissed him on the forehead.

Frank just stood there with red lipstick kissed on his forehead, looking totally confused.

"Come on Frank, it's so simple. Think about it." She pushed him into her leather desk chair and spun him around, forcing him to look out the window to the city below.

"The Republican and Democratic candidates are already

established, written in stone, waiting to be elected. What about those poor souls who aren't interested in being a Democrat or a Republican? What happens to them?" she asked.

She spun him back around and looked him in the face.

"You know what happens? They give up. They don't belong. Their ideas don't matter. So, they disappear into the political system as unknowns, taking their vote with them, hoping one day they'll be heard," she said.

She spun Frank back, facing the window again.

"Look at them, the ones you can't see, down there waiting for a chance to be heard. They're frustrated as hell, because they're tired of waiting," she said. "Waiting for a political system that let's them vote for someone they believe in and won't stamp them with a label."

Janet leaned forward this time and whispered in Frank's ear.

"Let's give it to them Frank. Let's put together a political reality television show that gives Americans the opportunity to choose the Independent Presidential candidate. We give them the opportunity to elect a President who's totally independent from the rest of the candidates, one that belongs to them."

She was making sense now, and Frank liked what he was hearing, but there were still a few more things that needed to be work out. He just sat there and let her work her magic.

"You know what else Frank, the Whitehouse can't touch us," she continued. "They can't touch us or our FCC licenses. That would put them in a very bad position. I believe it's called political harassment."

Janet walked to the center of her office and then turned and looked at Frank.

"If corporate America can use reality television to pick future executives to run huge organizations, then why can't Americans use reality television to pick future Presidents to run our country," she asked.

"Suppose we do focus the attention of Americans toward the Independent Presidential candidate, and the majority rally around this person. Where does this leave the Republican and Democratic candidates?" asked Frank.

"Back in the previous millennium where they belong," she answered. "Instead of sitting in line smugly waiting for their position in the Whitehouse, they'll have to crawl out of their political caves and actually prove they can do something for once. That's what those people out there are trying to tell us. They want to get back into the game again. They want a different system of voting."

"Okay, we create a political reality television show that gives Americans the opportunity to elect an Independent presidential candidate based on how well this candidate performs various tasks that we create, correct?" asked Frank.

"That's right," said Janet.

"What do we call it?" asked Frank.

Janet began pacing again.

"Let's see, it's a new voting system created during the beginning of a new millennium," she said. "It's by the request of Americans for America. Something in this has to work. American, America, voting, millennium, American, millennium, American..."

She snapped her fingers again and shouted, "I got it! We're creating a new America during a new millennium, therefore we call it *Millenica*," she said.

"I like it," said Frank. "We're creating a new America during a new millennium. It has a ring to it. What's most important is it's going to be bigger than *The Candidate Elect* could ever have been, and the Whitehouse can't touch us. Fantastic!"

Frank was completely satisfied with the new idea and he was ready to take it to the corporate officers.

"You did it again young lady, "he said. "I'm not going to have any trouble selling *Millenica* to the brass upstairs. You and Robert start merging the two shows together. We're going to have to create a new timeline that will synchronize with the 2012 Presidential Election. Most important, I don't want to lose any of our contestants, but we have to make sure they're up to the challenge."

"I understand. Robert and I will get right on it," said Janet and she took a tissue and wiped the lipstick off his forehead.

As Frank was leaving her office, he stopped at the door, turned and looked at Janet.

"You're quite a woman, Ms. Kendrick," he said. "Why don't you run for the position of President? Just now, it sounded like you know more about what the people want than those who claim to represent us."

Janet sat at her desk, clasped her hands together and leaned forward.

"Someone has to separate the good guys from the bad guys Frank. That's what you and I are for. That's why we're here. We handle politics in a different way, the right way. We don't let it handle us," she replied.

Chapter Eighteen
A New Direction

After presenting *Millenica*, the corporate officers were excited and relieved to know that the pressure from the Whitehouse would be eliminated and their political reality television concept could continue. Frank asked for their assistance with securing the Independent Presidential Candidate position, which they eagerly accepted.

The timeline was next. If all fourteen contestants agreed to perform and the show was synchronized with the 2012 Presidential Election, then the contestants would be introduced during the first week of March, 2012. The competition would begin the second week of March with the first elimination taking place at the end of that month. Eliminations would occur every two weeks after that until the contestants were narrowed down to the final three, which would occur by the end of August, 2012. Then, the Primary Election would occur in September. During that time, the final two contestants would put together their campaign plan of action and present them for elimination at the beginning of September. Thus, by November, 2012 the first place winner would move on as the 2012 Independent Presidential Candidate and the second place winner would become that candidate's nominee for Vice President.

Frank issued the timeline to Janet and she and Robert set up a meeting with the contestants. Prior to the meeting, Janet wanted to meet with Simon. Being the host of the show, she felt he should be the first to know what was happening. Robert went on his way to organize the contestants and Janet called Simon to her office.

"Come in Simon. Oh, you brought Richard with you," she said.

Janet got up from her desk, walked over to where the two men were standing and analyzed Richard's attire.

"Nice tie, Armani?" she asked.

"Yes it is," answered Richard. He then did the same to her.

"Great shoes, Prada?" he asked.

"Is there anything else?" she replied with a smile. "Please, have a seat."

As they made themselves comfortable, Simon made a desperate attempt to change the fashion conversation.

"I hope you don't mind if Richard joins us. I thought if I'm supposed to have another makeover, he should be in on it," he said.

Janet looked at Simon and then gave out a little laugh, "No, we're very happy with your Political Terminator image and we're not going to change it. Actually, the show is heading in a new direction and I wanted to go over the changes with you before we meet with the contestants."

"New direction?" inquired Simon.

"Changes?" asked Richard.

"Yes, due to some negative political side effects from the Whitehouse, we decided to eliminate the assistant to Vice President position," said Janet.

"What?" exclaimed Simon.

"How can you have a competition without a grand prize?" asked Richard.

"We thought our grand prize was becoming too limited for this scale of competition, so we came up with something much better," replied Janet. "As we're speaking, the corporate officers are making it possible for us to enter the winner of our show as the 2012 Independent Presidential Candidate."

"Presidential? Are you serious?" asked Simon.

"You mean the winner could become the President of the United States?" asked Richard.

"Is that possible?" asked Simon.

"All we need to do is secure the position, and the brass upstairs hasn't let us down yet," said Janet. "They'll think of a way to make this happen. In the meantime, we need to find out if all fourteen of our contestants will participate in the competition. We need all of them to stay in the race, because it affects the timeline of the show. I'm afraid, once they hear the stakes have gone up, they may quit. Simon, I'm going to need your help to keep our contestants in the game."

Richard turned and said, "Alright Simon, this is what you've been waiting for."

"I don't understand. What can I do to help? What do you mean, this is what I've been waiting for?" asked Simon.

"How soon they forget. Let's see, I remember about a year ago, there was this old political science professor who was stuck in a rut," said Richard. "This guy had been teaching for many years and was getting close to retiring, but he never gave up this dream he had. You know, I think I saw him on *The Kimberly Cross Show* recently. He mentioned something to her about wanting to be a part of creating a President of the United States. Let's see, now who was that?"

Richard began tapping his finger on the side of his head, pretending to remember something. Janet gave him a big smile as he did so. Simon looked at both of them, expressionless, not knowing what to say.

"Come on Simon, now's your chance," said Richard. "Make that dream happen. Be a part of the process that creates a President. Tell those contestants what they'll be giving up if they drop out now. Make them want to be a part of something wonderful, as much as you do. You can do it, I know you can."

"You're right Mr. Weeks. You're a good manager and a good friend. Ms. Kendrick, when do we meet with the contestants?" asked Simon.

"In about half an hour," replied Janet.

"I'll be there." Simon stood up, shook hands with Janet and left her office. Richard wasn't far behind, but Janet stopped him before he left.

"We never get the opportunity to see each other. I just wanted to say thank you," she said.

"For what?" asked Richard.

"For your college project, for meeting with me in Boise, for the show's concept, for being Simon's manager, and for what you did just now, I owe you so much. You don't know how grateful I am," said Janet.

Richard could tell that Janet's comment was sincere.

"Ms. Kendrick," started Richard.

"Janet," interrupted Janet.

"Janet," Richard said with a smile, "you don't know how pleased I am to see how far my idea has gone. Who could have imagined it would have become a popular television show and then grow into an actual presidential election? As for Simon, look how much he's progressed within a year. He looks ten years younger, he's become America's favorite reality TV show host, and he's asked me to be his manager. You know, a year ago, I almost transferred out of his political sciences class, because I thought his style of teaching and class curriculum were outdated."

Richard paused and then said, "Look at him now. He's having the time of his life and he has the opportunity to turn his dream into reality. It's amazing."

"If given the opportunity, some people can do amazing things," said Janet.

"Well, I better get going. Simon and I should go over what he's going o say to the contestants," said Richard.

"That sounds like a good idea," said Janet.

With that, Richard turned and walked out of the office.

Time had come to meet with the contestants. All fourteen were assembled in the same studio where the interviews were filmed for the show. John, Priscilla, Edward and William stayed close together. Robert greeted everyone as they arrived, but did not disclose the reason for the meeting. Everyone was talking amongst themselves when Janet and Simon walked in. Shortly after, Richard entered and stood next to Robert.

"May I have your attention Please, I have an announcement to make," shouted Janet as she walked in front of the group. "I want to thank all of you for showing up on such short notice. What I'm about to tell you is very important and I want you to listen very carefully."

Janet paused, looked at Simon for a moment and then went on.

The Candidate Elect has been cancelled and the assistant to Vice President position has been eliminated," she announced. This brought on the sounds of whispering among the surprised contestants.

"The political reality television concept has become extremely successful and very popular to our television audiences," continued Janet. "To keep up with the demand, we had to do a bit of restructuring. Therefore, we're in the process of creating another show with the same concept that doesn't need assistance or approval from the Whitehouse. You could say, we've gone independent."

Janet paused again, waiting for a response, but all she received were bewildered faces.

"The new show is called *Millenica*. It was given that name because its purpose will be to create a new America during a new millennium and the grand prize for *Millenica* will be..."

Janet paused again and there was absolute silence. It was as if time has stopped for that moment.

"The Independent Presidential Candidate position for the 2012 Presidential Election!" shouted Janet.

There were mixed emotions of joy and fear on the faces of the contestants.

"President of the United States?" asked one contestant.

"Is this a joke?" asked another.

All the contestants started talking at once and Janet gave them a few minutes to let the news sink in.

"Everyone, please, this is not a joke," she assured them. "The winner of *Millenica* will be given the opportunity to run for the Independent Presidential Candidacy and the runner up will be that person's Vice President Nominee. At this time, I need to know if anyone wants to leave the show. You've all been great contestants, so please think abut your decision very carefully."

The contestants began talking to each other and it appeared that most wanted to continue, but there were four contestants that didn't want to take the challenge. Janet walked over to Simon.

"Simon, I need you now. It looks like there are four

contestants getting ready to walk. Do what you can and get them to stay," she said.

Simon nodded and walked to the front of the group. At first he appeared nervous and looked over at Richard for support. Richard simply nodded his head and gave Simon the thumbs up. That was all it took. Simon took a deep breath and then spoke to the group with confidence.

"I know some of you may be feeling a bit overwhelmed by the news you've just heard, and I don't blame you," he said. "If you think about it, you've been given a great opportunity to further yourselves in your careers. Perhaps some of you don't want to be President of the United States, but if you quit now, you'll be giving up an excellent opportunity. If you stay in the game and progress through the challenges, you'll be recognized all around America as that person who went for the presidency. The farther you go, the more you'll be remembered. Look at all the artists, singers, and designers who worked their way through reality television competitions and created their own businesses. Some of them became very successful, and they weren't even the winner of the show. They did remain in the competition and America noticed their talents as well as their passion to succeed. If anything, please stay in this game for yourself. I can't stress how much of a wonderful opportunity you're being given right now. Don't run from it, embrace it and see how far it will take you."

Richard walked over to Simon, patted him on the back and said, "Good job Terminator."

His speech had done it and the tone had changed within the group. Robert and Janet walked over to join Simon and Richard and they listened to the comments being said by the contestants.

"You know, he's right. Some of those contestants went on to make it big," said one contestant.

"Even the really bad ones went on to make commercials. People loved them," said another.

The Pilgrim Colony Contestants held their own conversation.

"So, are we going to stay in the game?" asked John.

"William and I are," said Edward.

"Why not?" said Priscilla. "We've come this far. So, the road just got a little bumpier. I'm with Simon. Let's see how far this adventure is going to take us."

"I guess it's unanimous," said John and then he turned to Priscilla. "Besides, I wouldn't mind having you as my Vice President."

"Who elected you President? Get in the backseat buster, because I'm driving this car all the way to the Oval Office," said Priscilla.

By the end of the meeting, all individuals had agreed to continue as contestants for the new political reality show, *Millenica*. Janet returned to her office and gave Frank the good news. Securing the Independent Presidential Candidacy position was all that was left to do.

The President was monitoring the activities of the network and he told his Whitehouse staff to sideline any applications or permit requests that appeared questionable from the network. As time went by, the corporate officers realized that in order to meet show deadlines, they would have to become a little more creative.

Chapter Nineteen
Listen to Your Mother

Simon's speech did the trick and the contestants were eager to start the competition, but the list of performance tasks was still in the process of finalization. The network decided they should find out what their television audiences thought a future President should be held accountable for and ideas received would be utilized for creating performance tasks for the show. With the shadow of terrorism still in America and the war lingering in the Middle East, it was assumed that people would primarily focus on maintaining the safety of our country. When suggestions came in, they showed that safety was a concern, but in order to create a stronger country, other issues took precedence.

People wanted substitutes for oil and gasoline as well as the modes of transportation that utilized them. Because of the increase in pollution, the decrease in our ozone layer, and the extreme changes in weather conditions, people understood that if we continued to utilize these items for another century, the outcome would be detrimental to our health and the earth.

People wanted to reinvent farming. They felt that we were

wasting valuable land on golf courses, shopping malls, mega hotels and amusement parks. They also wanted to stop spending money on imported food when we could grow our own. They wanted America to nurture its lands, turn it back into farmlands and pay farmers a good wage, so we could feed our people, eliminate starvation and possibly export our food products for a profit.

People felt there were too many cutbacks in our educational system. They wanted to create a superior teaching staff that could utilize tools needed to educate our children and conquer our own national challenges. This could be done by lowering college tuitions, increasing salaries and wages for teachers and providing the proper teaching apparatus.

People thought current programs regarding medical care, retirement, housing, employment, health and nutrition were adequate, but needed more attention.

Finally, and most important, people wanted to control the national debt. They were tired of waiting for our country to go bankrupt. They knew that it wouldn't take an act of war to take over America. All that was needed was a well organized corporate buy out. It happened to the Native Americans, why couldn't history repeat itself? Americans wanted less national spending and a focus on creating more national revenue.

"It was the middle of October, 2011, and even though the network was compiling a list of performance tasks for the contestants, they still hadn't received approval for the grand prize. The corporate officers were being told that an application for the Independent Candidacy needed a name to go with it. "To be announced," did not qualify as a candidate.

"Well Frank, where are we with our request for candidacy?" asked Janet.

"The same place we were four weeks ago," replied Frank. "We

pissed off the President and he'd doing everything he can to keep *Millenica* from going on the air. We're filling out the paperwork, but I'm sure it's going straight to the silver presidential shredding machine and flushed down the gold presidential toilet."

"That's what I thought. So how do we get around this?" asked Janet.

"If I knew, I would have done it four weeks ago," said Frank.

"My mother had a saying. I didn't understand what it meant until now," said Robert.

"What is it?" asked Janet.

"If Mohammad can't go to the mountain, then bring the mountain to Mohammad," replied Robert.

Janet looked at Robert and thought about what he said.

"What's he talking about?" asked Frank. He appeared to be irritated at the unusual comment.

Robert looked at Janet and said, "If the candidacy position can't be applied to the contestants, then have the contestants apply for the candidacy position,"

"Right, have each contestant apply separately as an Independent Presidential Candidate," shouted Janet.

"Can we do that?" asked Frank.

"Sure we can, because each independent candidate application will have a name attached to it," said Janet. "As the show progresses, contestants will be eliminated and dropped from the candidacy. We can have a copy of their application and stamp it "DENIED" as they leave the show. By the end of the competition, there will be just one Independent Presidential Candidate left. We can do it Frank, now go upstairs and get the ball rolling."

Janet walked over to Robert, placed both hands on the cheeks of his face, and gave him a big kiss on his forehead.

"That's for listening to your mother," she said.

Frank turned and headed out the office door.

"He's a genius, and absolute genius," he said. "I'll let you know what happens. Get the list of performance tasks completed by the end of the week."

Frank had gone from the office to the elevator while he was talking. The elevator doors closed by the time he finished his sentence.

Chapter Twenty
A New Generation of Voters

It was the end of November, one year before the 2012 Presidential Election, and the network had all the contestants registered as Independent Presidential Candidates. It wasn't difficult for them to qualify, since they had already gone through the network's meticulous screening and interviewing process.

Millenica was being promoted as the first American political reality television show with a grand prize being the Independent Presidential Candidacy. This was a show for the people, a show for those who didn't want to register as Democrat or Republican, but did want a candidate they felt confident could lead our country. This was a show for people who wanted to see a presidential candidate perform and not just promise. This was a show for people who wanted to create a new America during a new millennium.

The news reached the media that the Whitehouse had withdrawn their generous offer of assistant to the Vice President from the network, which in turn inspired the new political reality television show called *Millenica*. The question everyone wanted to know was, why? Had the network done something wrong? Was it because of the *American Voting System Poll*? Did the President believe that a new voting system would be the downfall of America? This time, the questions had to be answered and the President agreed to hold another press conference. Remembering how chaotic the last press conference became, the President and his staff decided it would be better to carefully control the press room. They would create a list of questions and answers and then place staff members portraying reporters in the conference room to which the President would direct his attention.

The President and his staff gathered to create the list.

"Mr. President, it would be best if we started by answering why we withdrew the position from the show."

"That's right, first we were all for it, then we withdrew it, why?"

""That's why we're here people," said the President. "Now let's come up with some answers."

"How about, due to the escalating situation in the Middle East and the high level of security needed to sustain our position, it was decided that now would not be a good time to bring civilians into the Whitehouse."

"That sounds like it might work, and it may even take the subject off the show and sidetrack questions to conditions in the Middle East," said the President. "I don't like the word civilian. It sounds demeaning."

"Let's call them, unauthorized personnel."

"Good, conditions have escalated to where it would be unwise to have unauthorized personnel in the Whitehouse. Okay, next question," said the President.

"What's the Whitehouse's position on *The American Voting System Poll*, for or against?"

"Everyone here knows my opinion, but what's the Whitehouse's opinion?" asked the President.

"Let's acknowledge the poll and bury it in analysis. Something like, the poll has brought to our attention that adjustments to the current voting system have been deemed necessary by citizens of the United States. Adjustments will not be hasty, but this subject will seriously be taken into consideration creating further investigations through a series of analysis."

The President paused for a moment, thought about the answer and then he said, "You guys sure earn your income. I know you answered the question, but I have no idea what you said. Okay, next question."

"What are the President's thoughts about *Millenica*?"

"That one's easy. It's a network reality television show using Hollywood to exploit the American Presidential Election," said the President.

"Okay, but how about we tone that down a bit by saying it's simply a reality television show that represents a new generation of voters seeking their own political existence and it shouldn't be taken any more seriously than that?"

"A new generation of voters, what's this country coming to when people think they can elect a President through a television show?" asked the President.

"That's what this press conference is all about Mr. President. You're going to get this new generation back on track and into the real world. Your job is to set them straight."

"Imagine what would happen if we strayed from the political proceedings we've so carefully built over the centuries."

"It's only a television show Mr. President, a fad that will disappear with the ratings drop."

"Damn right! Now, let's finish this list and get this conference over with," said the President. "We have a crisis in the Middle East that needs more attention than this nonsense."

The President and his staff completed the list and held their press conference. The plan to control the room proved successful and this time, the conference ran in favor of the President. However, his plan to set the new generation straight and gain their support backfired and it showed in their response. Citizens felt pushed aside, let down, ignored and frustrated. His actions caused the new generation of voter to retaliate. They started forming independent groups, making it perfectly clear that they weren't going to wait any longer. Politically, they were going to be heard.

Chapter Twenty-One
Let the Show Begin

The request to be in the audience was enormous and the producers of *The Kimberly Cross Show* had to find new accommodations to hold the large number of people who wanted to attend the show. An unusual occurrence was that most of the requests came in the form of groups, some large and some small. Some represented elementary schools, high schools, college fraternities and sororities. Some represented small businesses, hotels, hospitals, grocery stores, and restaurant chains. From limousine services to fire stations, the group requests kept coming in. Some individuals simply created their own group names to show their independency. The producers wanted to work this group theme into the show somehow, but they didn't know why it was happening.

A large warehouse was selected that could hold up to two thousand five hundred people. The audience seats were arranged coliseum style, similar to that of a football stadium, and the stage was smack dab in the middle of everyone. Special sound systems, lighting equipment, huge video screens, camera equipment and set designs were purchased to make this event spectacular. The premier of *Millenica* was coming to *The Kimberly Cross Show* and the producers of both shows weren't about to spare any expenses.

It was March, 2012, and the enormous warehouse had been transformed into a magnificent television show setting that was filled to capacity. The premier of *Millenica* was about to go on the air. Audience members brought their banners, signs and posters, each representing their own groups.

The lights dimmed and the audience went silent. Four huge video screens that loomed overhead came to life, giving everyone in the audience a perfect view of the center stage. Suddenly, the theme music boomed and a spotlight beamed sown on the entrance to the stage. The audience burst into cheers when their female idol, Kimberly Cross, immerged with her arms in the air. They waved their banners, signs and posters all vying for her attention. Dancing colored lights engulfed the center stage and the cameras zoomed in on Kimberly as she ran to her mark. Once situated, the stage lights came up and Kimberly greeted her audience. She announced some of the groups by their identifying signs and then had them stand and be recognized.

Keeping the energy going, Kimberly announced the premier of everyone's favorite political reality television show. One by one, she introduced the contestants to the stage, saving the Pilgrim Colony Contestant for last. She announced William and Edward as the Mayflower Pilgrim Colony Contestants and then John and Priscilla as the Millennium Pilgrim Colony Contestants. Kimberly finished up by introducing Janet as the executive producer of the show, Simon as The Political Terminator and host of the show, and Richard as the college student who inspired the idea for the show. With everyone introduced and comfortably in their place on stage, Kimberly started the discussion.

"First, I have to say thank you for creating this wonderful

concept," she said. "I had my largest viewing audience and largest audience response, ever, to the special we did on *The Candidate Elect*. You should all be proud of yourselves, look at the size of this audience.

Spotlights shined on the audience as they clapped.

"Thank you Kimberly. We're all very proud of what we've accomplished with *Millenica* and our political reality television concept," said Janet.

"Why has it become so popular?" asked Kimberly. "It's literally taking over America."

"It started as a simple television show and then it became a voice for the people," replied Janet. "Our network did an analysis on who is most involved with political reality televisions and we found that the majority of viewers are currently in the form of groups, all kinds of groups. The Independent Candidacy Position and the number of contestants participating in *Millenica* is the cause for these different independent groups. We believe as the show progresses and contestants are eliminated, the groups will begin merging into one single independent candidate support group. As for why the show is so popular, you can thank the President for that. The people are telling us, they want someone or something different in the Whitehouse."

The audience started clapping.

"I heard he made a lot of people angry when they found out he planted his Whitehouse staff in the conference room area. Tsk, tsk, tsk, shame on you Mr. President." The audience laughed as Kimberly waved her finger into the television camera.

"Welcome back Simon, it's good to see you again. What do you think is causing all this *Millenica* mayhem?" asked Kimberly.

"You mean, besides my good looks and charming personality?" replied Simon.

Kimberly leaned forward, winked at Simon and said, "That's what I thought too."

"Seriously, I believe that a change is taking place," said Simon.

"A change, what kind of change would that be?" asked Kimberly.

"As you know, I've been teaching political science for many years and I've noticed students have lost interest in politics, mostly because they think the current system can't be changed and it's outdated and boring," said Simon. "Students between the ages of eighteen and twenty-five make up quite a large group. You watch, I guarantee you'll see an increase in registered student voters this year. *Millenica* is the change they've been waiting for to put the fun back in voting as well as create an immediate change in how we may do things."

All the students in the audience clapped and waved their banners.

"I think it'll be more than just students finding their way back to the voting booths this year," said Richard.

"Coming from the one who created this concept from his political science class project, how do you see things progressing Richard?" asked Kimberly.

"I agree with Janet and Simon, it's the people of America telling us they want something different in the Whitehouse and a change in the way our government does things," said Richard. "*Millenica* will be the vehicle to take us there. That's why I think there's going to be a big increase in the number of registered voters this year for the Independent Candidacy."

The audience clapped and cheered.

"It sounds like you're right Richard," said Kimberly. "It all depends on this diligent group of potential political leaders we have joining us today. Some I've already met and I'll be speaking with them later, but I have a question for the others. Doesn't it make any of you nervous knowing you may be the future President of the United States? Are you ready for something like this?"

The contestants looked at each other to see who wanted to answer Kimberly's question. Tyler Eastland was the first to respond.

"If you can't take the heat, get out of the kitchen," he said. "We all entered knowing we'd be in the Whitehouse somewhere, so now it's going to be in the President's seat."

"When things changed with the show, some of us were a bit nervous at first," said Tiffany Bates. "Then we realized that this is an excellent opportunity for all of us. We had to get it into our heads that we're actually running for that big position of President of the United States. The only difference is, instead of campaigning, we'll be performing."

"It's all in how well we perform," said Chris Flanagan. I know I'm ready."

"Where are my pilgrims?" asked Kimberly and the four raised their hands.

"You seem to be the people's choice to win. How do you think this is going to affect your performance? Do you feel pressured to win?" she asked.

"It's more like we're getting added support," said John, "not only from each other, but from the people of America."

"I agree," said Priscilla, "since the first interview, we found we had something wonderful in common. Then when we were on your show, we bonded like family."

"The camaraderie connecting the four of us feels great and will probably be the factor that takes us to the Whitehouse," said Edward.

"At least two of us," said William.

"That's right, President and Vice President," said Kimberly.

"Like Chris said, it's all based on how well we perform," said John.

"We discussed that on my show. Do any of the contestants know what the performance tasks are?" asked Kimberly.

"Topics for performance tasks were left up to our television audience," said Janet, "and they compiled a list of ten concerns they feel need immediate attention. The list of concerns was shared with the contestants. At this point, contestants only know what the topics are. They don't know what the tasks are."

"Do you think we can persuade Janet into sharing some of those concerns with us today?" coaxed Kimberly.

The audience shouted, "Tell us Janet!" They shouted over and over, but Janet just smiled and waited for them to quiet down.

"And spoil the surprise, no, you're just going to have to wait and watch the show," she said.

Kimberly went on with the show asking *Millenica* related questions and discussing possible topics. She included time for her audience to ask questions too. The show was coming to an end and Kimberly finally asked the question she had been patiently waiting to ask.

"Do you think the President is watching?" she asked.

"I'm sure he is," replied Janet.

"Is there anything you'd like to say to him?" asked Kimberly.

"Yes, I would," said Janet and then she turned and looked directly into the camera. "Never say never and nothing lasts forever. Those are words to live by Mr. President. Sometimes, change is good."

The cheering and clapping from the audience was deafening.

The President was sitting alone in his Whitehouse bedroom watching the show. Janet's statement forced him to get up and walk over to his desk. He pulled out an address book, flipped through the pages and then picked up the phone. His face held a loathsome scowl as he dialed the number.

"Hello. Yes, get me Agent Davis."

Chapter Twenty-Two
Denied by Design

The premier of *Millenica* put everyone in the voting mood. Diehard Democrats and Republicans sneered at the so called fanatical Independent activists. A new sense of political competition was in the air. It was going to be a horserace this year, a 2012 political horserace.

The network created a special set for the show. It resembled a typical presidential campaign room with everything decorated in red, white and blue enhanced with an abundance of balloons, hats and streamers for everyone. A large stage sat in the back center of the set. On the wall of the stage were presidential posters of each contestant with their framed candidacy application next to it. In the event a contestant was eliminated from the show, a sign would be placed in the frame that exhibited, in big bold letters, the word "DENIED." This indicated that the contestant's application had been denied and they were to be withdrawn from the candidacy. In front of the stage was a large round table, with a chair for each contestant and one for the Political Terminator. At the end of each task, the contestants would be seated at the round table where they would discuss the details of their performance tasks. At that point, the Political Terminator would announce the eliminated candidate and the "DENIED" sign would be placed in their application frame showing that the contestant had been withdrawn from the race.

During the second week of March, the contestants were working on their first performance task and the topic was fossil fuel. The people's main concern was that it was making our country too dependent on other countries. The performance task for the contestants was to find a fuel substitute within two weeks that would make this country less dependent on other countries. The contestants were divided into two groups with one team leader and it was made clear that the team leader would be held accountable for the performance task.

The teams were filmed while they progressed through their tasks. Both teams worked well within their groups at discovering new sources of fuel, but when it came to the end of the task, the team that appeared to be leading, surprisingly came up short. That team leader was collecting valuable information on his laptop and somehow his information has been completely deleted due to a computer virus. There was no way to retrieve his information to complete the task, so he and his team came to the campaign table without a presentation. He gave every excuse he could, but it was understood that the team leaders were held accountable for the tasks and since his team failed to perform, he was eliminated by the Political Terminator, his application was denied, and he was withdrawn from the race.

Priscilla was the team leader for the winning team and she was awarded $10,000 that she could keep or use as a donation to her campaign fund. Her team presented a substitute fuel that was created from landfill garbage in the form of liquid methane and methane gas. Once a landfill reached its limit, it would be covered to allow decomposition. A methane refinery would be constructed while the garbage was decomposing and creating crude methane gas. Once the decomposition was complete, the crude methane gas would be pumped to the refinery where it would be turned into both liquid methane and methane gas that could be safely used as a fuel substitute. When the gas had been completely extracted, the soil would be removed and the site would be transformed back to a landfill for future crude methane gas. This endeavor would result in a never ending cycle of methane fuel, as long as we kept creating garbage. Most important, it would allow us to become less fuel dependent on other countries. Each team member performed various tasks during their research. Some worked as landfill employees while others worked in the refinery and their presentation was put together in the form of a documentary showing the process they went through to create their fuel substitute.

The second performance task began on April first and contestants were given two weeks to work on the topic of farming. People were concerned that we were wasting valuable farmland causing unnecessary spending on imported food products. The performance task for the contestants was to reinvent farming and make it more profitable as well as valuable to our country.

Again, two teams were created and the team leaders were to be held accountable for the performance task. Tiffany Bates was chosen to be a team leader and her team was in the lead as the performance task drew closer to the end. All of a sudden, Tiffany became very ill, placing her in the hospital and eventually falling into a coma. Doctors couldn't determine the cause for the illness, but suspected it had something to do with a persisting diabetic condition. Her tragic situation caused her team to lose focus on the performance task and they did poorly at the campaign table.

Tiffany had to be eliminated and withdrawn from the race, because the doctors could not estimate her time of recovery.

John Alden was the winning team leader for this task. He also received $10,000 that he could keep or use as a donation to his campaign fund. His team continued with the concept of turning garbage into gold and team members worked on a farm and performed various farming tasks to create their documentary.

Being a restaurant entrepreneur, John knew that the quality of food and beverage products began with the soil. During the first performance task, soil was removed from the methane refinery site to recreate the garbage landfill site. During the decomposition period, not only was crude methane gas being created, but the soil was being rejuvenated with vitamins and minerals creating dark, rich, valuable soil. This soil would be issued to farmers at a very low price and even donated to farms having difficulty maintaining their product due to poor soil. Once the methane refineries became abundant and rotated their pumping schedules on a yearly basis, rejuvenated soil would be issued to farmers on a yearly basis. An abundance of quality, low priced soil meant more farms with high quality farm products, and money saved from not having to feed the soil would be put back into the farm in the form of equipment and hired hands. Farms that donated food to charitable organizations, such as feeding the homeless, would be given extra tax benefits. Quality farm products would be sold at a good price to the people of our country and other countries as well allowing us to export more and import less and take our farming business out of the red and into the black.

The third performance task began the third week of April and the topic was on transportation. People were concerned that the amount of emissions from our current modes of transportation were destroying our ozone layer and polluting the Earth. People wanted a better invention other than the toxic emission spewing combustible engine.

The teams were divided and the leaders selected were William Bradford and Chris Flanagan. William drew from his computer transportation experience to assist with this technical task. While transporting computer equipment to Canada, William could see the ugly affects pollution was inflicting on the ecosystem and he noticed a difference its affects had in Canada compared to the United States. Canadian landscapes were exceptionally cleaner. William knew he needed new technology to win the performance task and he had connections in Canada with computer organizations that focused on mechanical transportation technology, so he packed up his team and flew them to Canada. Chris had the same idea about finding new technology, but flew his team to a different location, in a different direction. At this point, both teams were progressing along very well without any difficulties reaching their destinations.

Once in Canada, William met with the head of the transportation organization and inquired if he had any successful technological developments using liquid methane as a fuel. There had been successful experiments performed and the experts were more than happy to share their information. Team members were filmed as they participated in the demonstrations. The organization had invented a liquid methane fuel engine that utilized a heat resistant lubricant created from normal organic oils. The methane engine operated the same way as a gasoline engine, cost a little less to construct and looked similar in shape and size. The major difference was that it did not emit toxic fumes and the lubricating oil could be discarded or recycled as it was totally biodegradable. It was the first environmentally friendly methane fuel engine invented and was considered to be ahead of its time. Automobile manufactures looked at the engine as being too radical and therefore, did not invest. The organization was currently working on a substitute for diesel fuel, but they didn't want to share their findings as it was still in the experimental stage. William created his documentary and returned to the campaign table with his team.

Another unusual turn of events occurred when Chris returned to California from his previous location. He made it through the first airport without any difficulty, but when he went to claim his bags at LAX, he was stopped by an airport security dog. He was taken to a private room and his bags were searched and to his surprise, a small bag of cocaine was confiscated from one of his suitcases. While his team returned to the campaign table, Chris was taken to the police station and held for questioning. He couldn't explain how the cocaine got inside his suitcase other than it was planted there. Chris was placed in jail, where he had to wait for his day in court. In the meantime, he was eliminated as a contestant, his application was denied and he was withdrawn from the race. William became the winner of the third task with an award of $10,000.

Prior to the fourth task, John Alden called a secret meeting with the Pilgrim Colony Contestants. He was concerned about the unusual events that kept occurring on the show and he wanted to discuss it with the others.

"Listen, this may sound crazy, but I don't believe these situations are an act of fate," he said.

"I was thinking the same thing, but wanted to hear it from someone else," said William.

"What is it John? What's going on?" asked Priscilla.

"Don't you find it a little unusual how the contestants are being eliminated from the show? First, it was a computer virus, then a coma and now confiscated drugs. Eliminations haven't been based on performance, they're based on mysterious, unexplained, suspicious situations and I seriously believe these situations are being planned in advance," said John.

"You mean sabotage?" asked Edward.

"These occurrences are being designed for potential winners of each task and they're making the contestants look bad. I don't know why, perhaps to keep competent leaders from entering into the presidential election," said John.

"We're being denied by design," said William.

"And as we get closer to becoming potential winners, we'll be next," said Priscilla.

"You don't think this is a scheme cooked up by the network to boost their ratings?" asked Edward.

"*Millenica* doesn't need any help with ratings," said John. "Why would the network put their number one television show in jeopardy with the possibility of creating a scandal and ruining their reputation? No, it's not the network. Someone else has more to gain from this, someone who doesn't want a qualified contender entering the 2012 Presidential Election."

"The President?" asked Priscilla.

"It's too soon to point fingers, but I do want to make a suggestion," said John. "I think it would be wise, from this point on, for each of us to be very careful. We need to pay attention to everything going on around us and let each other know if something suspicious is happening."

"Sounds like a good idea to me," said William.

"Count me in," said Edward.

"Priscilla, I think it would be a good idea if you stay out of the limelight for a while," said John. "You were the one who started the show with the methane fuel concept and it's been used in each performance task in one form or another. You're the only one who's somehow involved in each task, making you the potential competition leader of the show."

"I agree," said Edward. "We don't' want you to disappear or have your reputation ruined. Besides, it's my turn up to bat, but I'm not playing just yet. Why don't we all just take a step back, blend into the background and let the other contestants become targets."

"I'm all for that," said William.

"Don't you think we should tell Janet?" asked Priscilla.

"She's a smart woman, I have a feeling she has her suspicions too. If we say something now, it could get blown out of proportion and the show could be cancelled, giving whoever's behind this, what they want," said John. "Let's let Janet take care of the show while we take care of each other."

"I think we'd better get back, someone may notice us missing," said Edward.

"Okay, but remember, watch out for anything suspicious," said John.

More and more viewers tuned in to watch *Millenica*. Some watched specifically for the dramatic surprise conclusion, but the majority tuned in to watch the contestants take on the challenging topics and conquer the concerns of the people. They enjoyed watching the contestants perform the tasks, getting right in the thick of things and thoroughly explaining how things worked. Everywhere you went, you heard people discussing the performance task documentaries. It literally became America's daily subject for discussion. It was also becoming apparent that political promises held very little weight. With *Millenica*, you had your question answered, knew that it could actually be done and saw the finished product. When a campaign commercial hit the airwaves showing a potential political candidate making another campaign promise, you'd hear viewers say things like, "Sure, let's see you do it first," or "What a joke, *Millenica* rocks!" Even diehard Democrats and Republicans stopped sneering at their

Independent colleges. They'd proven to be worthy political adversaries deserving some recognition, but total respect hadn't been earned quite yet.

It was August fifteenth and the Political Terminator had eliminated ten contestants. The Pilgrim Colony Contestants' plan to lay low had worked and they were the show's four remaining contenders. In approximately one more month, the 2012 Primary Election would occur and Frank Soars was in Janet's office discussing *Millenica's* timeline as the show was nearing completion.

"We're right on schedule," said Frank. "By the end of this month, we'll be down to our final three contestants. Then, during the beginning of September, those three contestants perform their final task, we eliminate one more contestant and announce the first place winner as the 2012 Independent Presidential Candidate and the second place winner as their nominee for Vice President. After that, they're on their way to the General Election."

"You did an excellent job keeping everyone on schedule Frank," said Janet.

"Let me tell you, it wasn't easy. All those strange situations happening to the contestants were a little scary," said Frank. "In the beginning, there was a coma and jail time for confiscated drugs, then a broken leg, a burning house, a car accident, children disappearing from their home, and how did Tyler Eastland end up on a plane to Saudi Arabia without a passport? We're still trying to get him back to the United States. I've never seen a television show that had so much contestant bad luck."

"It didn't seem to hurt the show. It actually increased our viewing audiences," said Janet.

"You're right, people do love drama," laughed Frank.

Janet got up from her desk, walked over to the window and gazed outside.

"Frank, you're right, there was too much bad luck for our contestants. I can't believe I'm going to ask you this, but I have to know and I want you to tell me the truth," said Janet.

Frank walked over to the window next to her.

"What is it?" he asked.

"Did the corporate officers create any of that bad luck for our contestants?" asked Janet.

"No, they didn't," he answered. "As a matter of fact, they were concerned about their safety and almost shut down the show. They're assisting Tiffany's family with the medical bills until she recovers from her coma. They're paying for Chris's legal fees to keep him from going to prison, and they're spending a fortune getting Tyler out of Saudi Arabia. No, Ms. Kendrick, they had nothing to do with any of that. We thought the contestants were doing it to each other, but how do you put someone in a coma?"

"Thank you Frank, I'm glad to hear that, but it also makes me uneasy," said Janet.

"Uneasy?" inquired Frank.

"I'm sure someone is behind this. Someone's been trying to shut this show down since the very beginning. Remember the missing information from the laptop? We're getting close to the end of *Millenica* with the Primary Election occurring right after. I'm getting a bad feeling Frank. Someone's going to do whatever they can to keep these two events from happening. I'm afraid someone's going to get hurt," said Janet.

"We can't stop the show now," said Frank. "*Millenica* is no longer just a reality TV show. Everyday, we receive hundreds of comments from people thanking us for what we're doing. Some say we put their faith back in the political system. Some tell us stories about how they've adapted the contestant's documentaries to their lifestyle or career. There are people out there buying stock in methane fuel refineries and futures in landfill soil farms. The documentary Edward did on the topic of education inspired a high school principle so much, she created her own student credit card system. The cards increase in value academic points. The better her students do in school, the more points they get on their credit cards. Then she went to a mall and had them donate clothes, school supplies, computers, and a bunch of material teenage crap. She took the stuff, created a school store and the only way students can purchase items from the store is by using their academic credit cards. She said her students respect what they buy because they had to work to earn it. The parents love it because their kids are learning how to make a living without having to get a job. They loved it so much, parents who have their own businesses started donating stuff to the school without being asked. The poorer students can depend on themselves and not their struggling relatives when they need to by school supplies or regular teenage stuff. Janet, this is a lot more to people than just a TV show. *Millenica* has become the vessel that's taking America out of the old millennium and into the new millennium. It's indirectly causing changes in the way America operates."

"Then we have to do something to protect the show and the contestants," said Janet.

"I'll bring it up to the brass tomorrow. They've become very attached to this show and the contestants. Don't worry, they'll think of something," said Frank.

"Okay, let me know what they come up with, and Frank, thank you for listening," said Janet.

"When my star executive tells me she has a problem, I'm going to listen," said Frank. "I'd better get going. I have to work on what I'm going to tell the brass tomorrow."

Shortly after Janet and Frank's meeting, William and Edward called a meeting with Simon and Robert. They were going to make an announcement on the air, and they wanted to let the network know before they did.

"We thought telling you in advance was the right thing to do," said William.

"What is it?" asked Simon. "Is something wrong?"

"As a matter of fact, everything couldn't be better, that's why William and I are withdrawing from the candidacy," said Edward.

"Withdrawing?" repeated Robert.

"If everything is fine, then why are you withdrawing?" asked Simon.

"Edward and I made a vow that we would see to it that John and Priscilla made it to the end of the competition. We meant it when we said that the two of them being in the Whitehouse was a sign," said William. "If for some reason, they had been eliminated, Edward and I would have continued on, but that's not the case."

"You're serious? You're both actually withdrawing from the candidacy?" asked Robert.

"Being descendents of the original pilgrims, William and I represent the old ways. John and Priscilla will go on to represent a new generation of pilgrims during this millennium, and now that they've reached their destination, there's no need for us to continue," said Edward.

"For things to change during this millennium there needs to be some new blood in the Whitehouse. Our government has become too anemic. Who knows, maybe the Whitehouse will be painted another color and given a new name, if you know what I mean," said William.

"What about the timeline and your contracts?" asked Robert.

"It shouldn't be hard for us to get out of our contracts," said Edward. "We simply say the show has become too hazardous to our health, a threat to our safety. Any lawyer who's been keeping up with the show will know what we mean. As for the timeline, you still have to determine who's going to be the Independent Presidential Candidate. Continue with the competition, delegate who's to be President and Vice President, and conclude the show with a campaign special for the Independent Candidates. William and I would like to donate our winnings of $20,000 to that event."

"That's very honorable," said Simon.

"Please, before you do anything, let me inform Ms. Kendrick of your intentions. I'm not sure how she's going to take it," said Robert.

"She'll understand. *Millenica* had so many twists and turns, it's only going to add to the drama. She'll make it work," said Edward.

"Do John and Priscilla know about this?" asked Simon.

"No, and we'd like it to be a surprise. That's why we waited to the last minute," said William.

"Thank you Mr. Bradford and Dr. Winslow. I appreciate you letting us know your intentions in advance. I must say, this is quite the surprise, but looking back on everything, it does make sense in a way. Once Ms. Kendrick hears all the details, I'm sure she'll understand," said Robert.

Robert turned and looked at Simon.

"Well Mr. Terminator, would you like to call Ms. Kendrick and let her know you just terminated two of her Pilgrim Colony Contestants from the candidacy?" he asked.

"Oh, no thank you Mr. Garcia. I think I'll let you have the honor, if you don't mind," said Simon.

Chapter Twenty-Three
Agent Davis

Robert explained the new turn of events to Janet and Frank Soars. They all agreed that William and Edward's decision would enhance the dramatic conclusion of *Millenica*, and they wasted no time created a special episode utilizing the show's TV campaign room as the setting. The special was a reunion of all the contestants, excluding still hospitalized Tiffany Bates and Saudi bound Tyler Eastland. Then, to everyone's surprise, William and Edward announced their withdrawal from the candidacy at the conclusion of the show. Priscilla and John tried to talk them out of it, but they remained firm and then came the generous donation of $20,000 to the campaign fund. Priscilla began to cry and ran over to embrace her loyal pilgrim guardians knowing they would soon be gone. John walked over and shook hands with his dedicated friends and gave each of them a heartfelt hug goodbye. John and Priscilla held each other as they watched William and Edward walk over to the presidential poster wall and place the "DENIED" sign in their application frames signifying their formal withdrawal from the candidacy. At that moment, the

Political Terminator, known for his rigid personality, performed an act that he'd never done before. As William and Edward were leaving the campaign room, he kneeled down in front of them and bowed his head with respect.

At the Whitehouse, the President watched the special episode of *Millenica* alone in the Oval Office. He sat with a look of disgust on his face. He loathed the idea that two reality TV show contestants were being given the opportunity to run the country. Immoral thoughts overwhelmed him as he contemplated various ways to keep that catastrophe from happening. He walked over to his desk, picked up a cell phone and made a call.

"We need to talk," was all he said. He patiently waited for about fifteen minutes and then there was a knock on the door.

"Come in," he shouted.

The door opened and in walked a mysterious looking individual. He had long black hair, wore sunglasses and was covered by a floor length gray trench coat. His face held a black mustache with a goatee and a scar on his right cheek. He walked over to the President and shook his hand.

"Good evening, Mr. President," he said.

"Take off that ridiculous costume," ordered the President.

The individual obeyed and proceeded to remove the hair, the sunglasses, the mustache and goatee, the trench coat and even the scar. Underneath his disguise was a totally ordinary looking human being. He had hazel eyes and short brown hair that was turning slightly silver at the temples. He was average height with an average build and looked to be around forty-ish. He could have been older, but his white Polo shirt, blue jeans and white tennis shoes gave him a more youthful appearance. There was absolutely nothing mysterious about the individual anymore. He looked as wholesome and ordinary as John Q. Public.

His name was Ryan Eugene Davis or Red to his good friends

and he'd been an agent for the C.I.A. for about seven years. He had acquired a questionable reputation due to the confidential assignments he was given, especially those issued by the President, and it appeared that the President was not happy with his current performance.

"I'm sure you didn't want anybody to recognize me," said Davis as he made himself comfortable in the plush Oval Office armchair.

"Why is *Millenica* still on the air?" growled the President. "You were told to take care of that mistake a long time ago."

"You've been watching my work. Since that show started, I've been creating unfortunate situations that would have closed down most places. Who would have thought so much bad luck could make something more popular," replied Davis.

"You're dealing with Hollywood you idiot. It's your fault that show is getting so much support from the people. They accuse me, but it's your pathetic attempts that created interest and made that show more popular in the ratings. You're lucky you didn't kill that Bates girl," said the President.

"Hey, I only wanted to make her sick and get her off the show," said Davis. "I didn't know she was diabetic. So, that stuff I slipped her didn't mix well with her medication. It's only a coma, she'll get over it."

"I want that show off the air and I don't want either of those contestants making their way to the Presidential Election," ordered the President. "Do I make myself clear?"

"Perfectly, however, now that the show is down to only two contestants instead of four, that's created a bit of a problem," replied Davis. "I'm going to have to be a little more extreme to get *Millenica* completely off the air. Do you understand?"

"I don't care how extreme you get. Just make sure whatever it is you do can't be traced back to you or the Whitehouse," said the President. "Do you understand?"

Davis stood, took his gray trench coat and formed it into a duffle bag, and then stuffed the articles from his disguise inside.

"What is it about that show? I mean, there have been Hollywood types that made it to the Whitehouse. What's the difference?" asked Davis.

"That show is a mockery of our entire political system. Those entertainers entered into the field of politics and worked hard to achieve what they did," said the President. "The presidency is not a prize. The presidency wasn't handed to them because they knew how to turn garbage into fuel. They followed in the same footsteps our forefathers did when this system was established in the seventeen hundreds. For centuries, the American political system has been protected and maintained and I'm not about to let some contemptible television game show ruin what Americans have fought for all these years."

"Okay, you're the boss. So you won't mind if someone tampers with the network's satellite and cable connections forcing the show to miss their critical election deadlines?" asked Davis with a sinister grin.

The President stood with his back to Davis and let out an impious smile that Davis couldn't see.

"Like I said before Agent Davis, I don't care how extreme, just get it done," he replied.

Chapter Twenty-Four
The Relocation

It was nine o'clock and most of the network staff had gone home for the evening. The only people remaining were the usual skeleton crew who kept things operating during the early morning hours. Preparations were being made for *Millenica*'s final performance task and Janet, Robert and Frank Soars had stayed late that night to brainstorm ideas for the conclusion of the show.

Suddenly, a large explosion shook the entire building. Office windows shattered and ceiling tiles fell. The lights went off for a moment and then the emergency lights came on. The building fire alarm noisily rang out through the hallways and office departments and then a recorded announcement ordered everyone to evacuate. The sounds of sirens could be heard racing toward the building from the streets below.

Robert was the first to reach the elevators, but it was too late. They had all automatically returned to the lobby forcing everyone to take the stairwell fire exit. Frank ran down the hallway and opened the fire exit door. He was greeted with the smell of smoke indicating that there was a fire somewhere in the building. Janet and Robert joined him and they entered the stairwell, Frank in front, then Janet, and Robert following behind. In their haste, they didn't notice that they were the only individuals in the stairwell, suggesting there were no other people occupying the upper floors.

As they descended the stairwell, the smoke increased. It clouded their vision, tore through their sinuses and burned in their lungs. They used clothing and handkerchiefs to cover their faces, but it did little good. When they reached the tenth floor, they saw the stairwell door was slightly open. A piece of computer equipment prevented it from closing and smoke was now pouring into the stairwell from the other side. Just as they ran past the door, a huge flame shot through the opening and burst up the stairwell right where the three had been seconds earlier. The door was closed enough to keep the fire from shooting down the stairwell. The heat and smoke intensified making their decent more excruciating, but after what seemed like an eternity, they finally made it to the exit, choking and gasping for air.

Paramedics greeted them and placed oxygen masks over their soot covered faces. They sat for a while to recuperate, and the paramedics recommended that the three be taken to emergency, but Janet and Robert turned down the recommendation stating that they were fine. Frank was having difficulty breathing, so he was immediately taken to the hospital in an ambulance.

When the fire was under control, Janet went up to one of the firefighters to find out what happened and if anybody had been injured.

"We still don't know what caused the explosion, but as far as we can tell at this time, it originated on the tenth floor," said the firefighter. "Luckily, nobody was injured because everyone was on the eighth floor or lower, except for you three. They all managed to get out of the building before the smoke and fire became a problem."

The firefighter paused for a moment and then said, "We don't know what caused the explosion, but it most likely wasn't an accident. What's on the tenth floor?"

Janet thought about what he said and replied, "That's the communications floor. It has computers, network cable connections and satellite links. Why do you think it wasn't an accident?"

The firefighter looked at Janet for a moment and then asked, "Is there anything on that floor that's highly explosive, like a fuel tank or high voltage electrical access lines?"

Puzzled, Janet replied, "No, all that is located below the fourth floor. Are you saying somebody intentionally did this?"

"That's what it looks like. There are two reasons for suspicion," said the firefighter. "First, there is nothing on that floor to have caused that intensity of explosion and second, all individuals, except you three, were below the tenth floor. I don't think you were meant to come out of that stairwell."

Janet stood speechless, thinking about what the firefighter told her. She looked down at her torn, soot covered clothes, reeking of electrical smoke fumes. Then she looked over at Robert who was sitting on the curb still using the oxygen mask to clear his lungs and she felt somewhat responsible for his discomfort. Then she saw Frank, in her minds eye like a vision, being wheeled into the hospital emergency room. He was unconscious and she was concerned about his heart condition. She remembered telling him that something bad was going to happen and she wondered if she could have prevented this whole situation from happening.

Then her vision took her deeper and she saw herself on a stage at a campaign rally and there were balloons flying and confetti falling. The room below was packed with people clapping and cheering, as if they were celebrating a victory. Out of nowhere, came the sound of a gun being fired. Immediately, the room became silent and everyone turned and looked up at the stage where Janet was standing. She looked down at the stage floor and saw a stream of blood, coming from nowhere, flowing towards her, forming a pool about two feet in front of her. She couldn't move, and she looked down at the people for help, but they just stood in silence, staring at her. The blood kept flowing and the pool grew larger and larger until it was almost touching her feet.

"Are you alright?" asked the firefighter, bringing Janet out of her state of premonition.

"Oh, yes, I'm fine. Thank you very much for all your help. I think I'll go over and see how Robert's doing," she said.

As she walked, it was clear to her that this wasn't an accident. None of the situations on the show were accidents and she realized how close they had come to being victims of someone's sadistic intentions.

She sat next to Robert.

"How are you doing?" she asked.

"I'm fine, just a bit shook up now that it's over. What did you find out?" asked Robert.

Janet paused and looked at Robert the same way the firefighter had looked at her, and then she said, "This wasn't an accident."

Robert sat speechless, waiting for her to continue.

"Somebody wants *Millenica* off the air and is going to do whatever it takes to make it happen," she stopped for a moment and remembered her premonition.

"But, is it worth someone's life to keep this show going?" she asked.

Neither said anything after that. They both sat quietly, looking at their marred network building as they watched the firefighters finish extinguishing the fire.

The next day, Janet and Robert went to the hospital to visit Frank before they went back to work. He'd been placed in a semiprivate room and was resting quietly in his hospital bed watching television waiting for updates on the fire.

"Hi Frank, how are you doing?" asked Janet.

"I'm fine," he replied. "They've got me under observation for a couple of days because of my heart. I'm okay though. So, how bad is it? They won't let me call anybody and there's nothing on the news. Will we have to shut down?"

"Well, the good news is, nobody was hurt," said Janet.

"Thank God, and the bad news?" inquired Frank.

"It's the tenth floor. What the explosion didn't damage, the water did," she replied. "I'm going to hear final estimates this morning, but they're saying that it will probably take four to five weeks to get our communication devices and satellite links back on line."

Four to five weeks? Do they know what caused the explosion?" asked Frank.

Janet and Robert looked at each other and then Janet said, "Not at this time."

"Four to five weeks, that means we won't be able to finish *Millenica*. Damn, we can't let that happen. Somehow, we have to keep that show going," said Frank.

"Frank, do you really think that's a good idea. Look at everything that's happened on the show and now with this explosion, perhaps it would be best if we take *Millenica* off the air," said Janet.

Frank was surprised at her suggestion.

"I'm sorry Janet, but I don't agree. Robert, tomorrow I want a meeting with you, Janet, Simon and his friend Richard, Priscilla,

John and see if you can get Kimberly Cross too," said Frank. "Between all of us, somebody may come up with an idea on how we can keep the show on the air."

"Certainly, Mr. Soars," replied Robert.

Janet suppressed the uneasy feeling she was holding inside. She thought perhaps, there may be a way to restructure the show and keep her bloody premonition from occurring.

Frank was released from the hospital the next morning with a clean bill of health. Robert had managed to get everyone together for the meeting including William and Edward. Kimberly couldn't leave her studio, but she was being included in the meeting via telephone conference call. The smell of smoke lingered in certain areas of the building creating an ominous reminder of the treacherous event that had occurred two days earlier. Everyone entered the conference room quietly, not knowing what to expect, but suspected they were about to be told they were out of a job. Robert had everyone take their seats and then Frank and Janet entered the room. Frank greeted everyone in an uplifting, energetic tone as he and Janet made their way to the head of the conference table. Janet took a seat, and Frank remained standing.

"As you all know," he began, "our satellite links and network communication equipment have been severely damaged and we're currently facing partial shutdown for approximately five to six weeks. We've managed to restore about fifty-seven percent of our networks programming using our backup emergency broadcasting equipment, but this leaves us without any devices to continue our number one television program, *Millenica*. It's still unknown what caused the explosion, but it's highly suspected that it was intentional. As a matter of fact, we've reached the conclusion that most of the unfortunate events that have occurred on the show were intentional. Therefore, I've brought you all together today because I believe this is one of the best teams this network's had in many years, and together, we're going to come up with a way to keep this show on the air, and continue as scheduled until we have an Independent Presidential Candidate for this upcoming election."

Frank leaned forward and said, "Kimberly, can you hear me?"

"Loud and clear Frank," broadcasted Kimberly's voice from the conference phone sitting in the center of the table. "I'm behind you one hundred percent."

"Great, now that everyone is up to speed, does anyone have any suggestions? Please keep in mind the obstacles ahead of us when making your comments," said Frank.

"Frank, you're always welcome to utilize my studio," started Kimberly. "*Millenica* has become such a powerful political tool and has gained the trust of people all around this country. It would be my honor."

"Thank you Kimberly, and don't think you weren't the first person I thought of, but I can't place your studio or your staff in jeopardy," said Frank.

"What if we use her studio as a home base?" suggested Robert.

"Home base?" inquired Frank.

"The show could be broadcasted from her studio, but it would originate from some unknown location, similar to a live news broadcast from some obscure place," said Robert.

"Or, we could act as if the show is being filmed here, when in actuality, it would be filmed at a different location, say San Francisco," said Edward.

"Or farther, how about Boise, Idaho?" said Richard as he looked at Simon.

"Of course, Mr. Sweets and Clearwater Cable," Simon snapped his fingers.

"Okay, what's Clearwater Cable?" asked Frank.

"I have a friend in Boise who's the station manager at a cable station called Clearwater Cable. His boss will jump at the opportunity to use his cable station as the location site for *Millenica*," said Richard.

"That sounds like a good idea," said Kimberly from the conference phone. "We can use our studio satellite links with the station in Boise. You create the show's studio set to look exactly like the one at your network, and nobody will know the difference, including your network terrorist."

"Using a small, unknown cable station is a good idea," said Priscilla. "We can keep our charade a secret longer than if we utilize a well know station. It will take the terrorist weeks to find the right location, and by then, the show will be over."

"Priscilla and I can go to Boise and complete the final performance task from there," said John.

"You know," said William, "that sounds like a good idea and it'll keep the two of them out of harms way. If the bad guys can't locate the station, they won't be able to find our contestants."

"Richard, is Clearwater Cable capable of handling something of this magnitude?" asked Frank.

"I'm almost positive, but let me follow up with my friend Joey. I'm sure he can make it happen," said Richard.

"Okay, then I think we have a plan. Richard is going to get back to us about Clearwater Cable and at the same time he can check on what type of satellite links they have so Kimberly can work with her people on setting up a broadcast connection. We create a duplicate *Millenica* set in Boise where our last two contestants will perform their final task and we broadcast it from the *Kimberly Cross Show* giving the impression we are filming from this network building. Any wrong doers with evil intentions will be detoured until the show is over keeping everyone safe and sound, and if there are no further comments or questions," Frank paused and looked at everyone giving them time to think, "then that's our plan and please, all those with follow up, keep Robert advised on your findings. In conclusion, I want to thank you all for another job well done. I knew you could do it."

The meeting was adjourned. Everyone stood and enthusiastically talked amongst themselves while they left the room and Robert finalized things with Kimberly over the phone. Frank asked Janet to stay behind, so he could talk privately with her.

"Janet, I noticed everyone had come kind of input except you. Is it because you still feel we should discontinue the show?" he asked.

"At this point, I don't know what to think," replied Janet. "Usually, my intuition leads me in the right direction, but something happened that night of the fire. I can't explain it. It's as if I had some kind of premonition that something extremely bad is going to happen if we continue with the show."

"A premonition, you mean you had a vision?" asked Frank.

"A vision, a dream, an out of body experience, I don't' know what to call it. I can't even explain what I saw, it doesn't make sense, but it does make me wonder if what we're about to do is the right thing," said Janet.

Frank sat quietly for a moment and looked at her.

"You know what bothers me the most?" asked Janet.

"What?" replied Frank.

"I'm apprehensive about continuing the show, because this vision happened after the explosion, not before, which makes me think that no matter what precautions we take at this time, the end result will still be the same," said Janet.

Frank told Janet not to worry and assured her that all the preventative measures planned for the show would prevent any further treacherous attempts against the contestants and the network.

Everyone busily went about completing their assignments and Richard was given airfare to Boise so he could personally meet with Joey. After they caught up on past and current events, Richard explained the reason for his visit and presented his request.

"You're serious, aren't you?" asked Joey, thinking he was being set up for a joke.

"As a heart attack," replied Richard.

"*Millenica* to be filmed at Clearwater Cable?" Joey pondered.

"That's right, the only question is, do you have space big enough to create an exact duplicate of the show's set? It's important that it's exactly the same," said Richard.

Joey paused, looked at Richard, and then told Richard to follow him. He led him to the back of the cable station and stopped in front of large, thick double doors that were locked with a large padlock. Joey took the keys he carried, released the padlock and swung open the doors revealing a vast amount of darkness and the smell of thick stale air. As Joey clicked on the hanging florescent ceiling lights, the sound it made echoed through the room. Richard stood with his eyes and mouth wide open. On the other side of the doors was a large empty warehouse. Camera equipment and television communication consoles were inside covered with sheets. The majority of the room was empty and everything was covered in year's worth of thick dust and cobwebs.

"What is this?" asked Richard.

"Remember, a long time ago, I told you Dale had big plans for this place. Well, this is it. When he purchased the cable station, he planned to create an adjoining television station, so he purchased this empty warehouse connected to it," said Joey. "Things didn't work out financially, so the warehouse was never used and Dale's too stubborn to sell it. Business has been getting better and I've make it a goal of mine, before I leave, to get things back on track for Dale so he can use this space as it was intended. He still has the TV equipment. It just needs to be put to use."

"This is perfect," said Richard. His voice and footsteps echoed as he walked across the dusty cement floor. "Do you think Dale will let us use it?"

"He's going to pass out when I tell him what you have planned. He'll probably make me a partner just to say, thank you," replied Joey.

"Don't forget, we need satellite link access for Kimberly Cross. It's going to be broadcasted from her studio," said Richard.

"Not a problem, Dale and I can work on that. I'm sure he already has something waiting in the wings," said Joey.

"Great! I'll have Robert contact Dale and they can work on the contract," said Richard.

Joey started laughing.

"What's so funny?" asked Richard.

"*Millenica, The Kimberly Cross Show*, and Clearwater Cable, which one of these things doesn't belong on that list? Remember our hike through the forest last summer and I asked what the station manager of Clearwater Cable could do for the manager of the Political Terminator? I guess that question was just answered," said Joey.

Richard started laughing and said, "I guess this proves we're meant to be friends. Who would have thought you had a TV station stashed away, waiting to bloom?"

Joey stood quietly for a moment, looking around the warehouse, picturing the lively transformation that would be occurring in a couple of days and then asked, "Did you ever think that class project of yours would amount to so much?"

"No, I didn't," replied Richard, "but I do know this, that class project of mine was just a seed. A lot more is about to take place, and everyone that gets involved feels it. I'm sure you've noticed a change in me and Simon. We're not the same people we were a year and a half ago. Now, it's your turn. You're meant to be a part of whatever's going to happen."

Joey turned, looked at Richard and said, "That sounds so occult."

Richard raised both his hands in the air like he was raising an invisible cape.

"Bla, bla, bla, ve vant you to become vone of us," he said in his best vampire voice. "That's vhy I flew all the vay up here, and boy are my arms tired."

The two laughed together and talked about things to come as they exited the warehouse. They plotted and planned as Joey turned off the florescent ceiling lights and closed the double doors, causing the sound to echo through the dark abandoned warehouse for what would be the last time.

Chapter Twenty-Five
The Winner

The adversities had been beaten. Tiffany Bates made a full recovery and was to be released from the hospital in a couple of days. Due to it being his first offense, Chris Flanagan's drug smuggling charges were dropped, but his behavior would be monitored for the next six months, and Tyler Eastland found his way back to American soil. Contracts between the network and Clearwater Cable were finalized as well as the satellite links between Boise's future television station and the Kimberly Cross studio. Through all assignments, a bond occurred between Robert and Joey. The two were a great team and they worked well together when it came to creating concepts and getting things done. Dale Brophy stood proud, watching his dream come true. His abandoned Clearwater television warehouse had been transformed into an exact duplicate of the network's *Millenica* studio set and preparations were being made to go on the air. John and Priscilla worked diligently on their final performance task which happened to be, controlling the national debt. They finished their presentations by the second week of September, three days before the Primary Election.

Frank Soars and Janet remained in California and continued operations at the network. Frank was in high spirits knowing he had beaten the odds and *Millenica* had reigned triumphant. Janet was having trouble sleeping at night. Her premonition had turned into a constant nightmare that would not allow her to sleep and as much as she wanted to be a part of the network's joyous event, her fatigue was getting the best of her. Frank suggested that she take a couple days off, at least until the show went on the air, but Janet knew it wouldn't do any good. She was becoming obsessed with the need to find the meaning to her premonition.

It was two days before the Primary Election, and network staff and Clearwater Cable staff worked in confidence to create a broadcasting illusion. The Political Terminator, John and Priscilla took their places, and then it as lights, camera, action. *Millenica* was filmed at Clearwater Cable, linked from satellite to satellite and broadcasted from *The Kimberly Cross Show*.

John gave his presentation first utilizing a small Pacific island where the people were completely self sufficient. He suggested that Americans simulate their lifestyles to reduce national spending. Priscilla went with a team concept. She presented a five year program utilizing all the previous winning contestant's concepts that already had been approved by the people. She stated that part of the program included reinstating all the previous contestants and putting them to work in the Whitehouse as her advisory staff and then she concluded her presentation with a powerful speech.

"Before the sun grows dark and cold. Before a stray asteroid crashes into the face of our planet. Before the Earth's core hardens and turns the world we know into a vast wasteland. Before all that, what is the fate of this world and humanity?"

"We are currently creating negative conditions that could very well annihilate the human race completely. Pollutants we've produced within the last century are generating dangerous weather conditions as well as the advanced stages of melting polar icecaps. Wars between countries have produced enough nuclear weapons to obliterate eight billion lives, and there are only six billion people on this planet."

"The time has come for everyone to stop thinking separately as countries and continents and start thinking as a world united. It's distressing to think that, because of politics, religious beliefs, and greed, we the people, will be the cause of our own destruction as well as destroying this beautiful planet we were given the opportunity to nurture."

"We have the power and technology to make positive changes for ourselves and this planet. The question is, will we?"

At *The Kimberly Cross Show* the audience stood and gave Priscilla a standing ovation. They cheered and whistled to let her know they supported what she said and what she wanted to do. The basis for her project was the result of American approved concepts to change their country and themselves. Priscilla was creating a new concept for politics. She was listening to the people and was giving them what they asked for.

The show ended with a landslide win for Priscilla Mullen and she became the Independent Presidential Candidate for 2012. John Alden, being the second place winner, became her candidate for Vice President.

The Millennium Pilgrims went on a voyage to the Whitehouse not knowing what to expect. They encountered dangerous situations and just like their diligent predecessors, they managed to pull through. The millennium Pilgrims were on their way to the Whitehouse bringing them fresh concepts, the support of the people, and new hope.

Chapter Twenty-Six
We See Red

Their plan had worked. Priscilla and John made it safely through *Millenica* and were looking forward to participating in the Primary Election. The two network challenges had been conquered, concluding the show without adversity and creating a "peoples choice" nominee for the Independent Candidacy. It appeared all was well and celebrations were in order, both at Clearwater Cable and at the Kimberly Cross studio.

"Ms. Kendrick, do you know what this means?" Frank has to shout over the music and joyous festivities. The confetti was falling, the balloons were flying, and the people were singing, but most important to Frank, the champagne was flowing.

"What does this mean?" shouted Janet.

With a big smile, Frank raised his glass of champagne and shouted, "You can stop worrying. The show is over and nobody got hurt."

Janet stood for a moment and thought about what Frank had said.

"You're right! You're absolutely right," she shouted with a smile, the worrisome expression she had been carrying around for days was finally melting away.

"There it is. I've missed that smile. Now why don't you get yourself a big glass of champagne and start celebrating with the rest of us?" said Frank. He was feeling no pain and he reached for another glass of champagne.

"That sounds like a wonderful idea, but first, I'd better get something in my stomach. I was so tied up in knots today, I forgot to eat," said Janet.

Frank looked around for Kimberly. He spotted her talking with a group of people and motioned for her to come over.

"Congratulations you two, could this show have gone any better? So, the next question now is, how are you going to top this next year?" asked Kimberly.

"Let's worry about that later. Right now, we have to get my executive producer something to eat. What can you suggest?" asked Frank.

"Well, of course, what are you hungry for?" asked Kimberly.

"Nothing extravagant, something small like a sandwich or a piece of cake," said Janet.

"This studio has a cafeteria. I think it's closed at this time, but I'll call security and tell them to let you in. I'm sure you'll find something there to eat," said Kimberly.

"That's perfect. Once I get something in my stomach, I promise, I'll be back to join the party," said Janet.

Kimberly walked Janet over to one of the studio security officers. He escorted her to the cafeteria and let her in. She told him that she wasn't going to be there long and requested he not turn on the lights. She could manage her way around with the lighting coming from the soda machines and refrigerated dessert displays. The security officer left and Janet made her way to the pantry where the cakes, pies and sandwich items were kept. What she didn't know was she wasn't alone.

Stunned, seeing that the show had been broadcasted as scheduled and the contestants met their Primary Election deadline, Agent Davis went to the *Millenica* network set. He wasn't sure how he was going to do it, but he still had a chance to keep Priscilla and John from making it to the General Election. He quietly entered the set from the back and saw network crew members running around, but there wasn't enough activity to prove the show had actually taken place there. Davis went to the tenth floor and saw that major repairs were underway; however, they weren't complete enough for *Millenica* to have been filmed at that location. He realized he had been duped and his next destination was the Kimberly Cross studio.

With all the festivities taking place, it wasn't difficult for Davis to make his way unnoticed into the studio. He went from floor to floor looking for Priscilla and John, but they couldn't be found. Finally, Davis ended up in the cafeteria at the same moment Janet was let in. He entered through the back and she was let in through the entrance. They had no idea the other was there.

Janet was looking over a Dutch apple pie and then she heard the ringing of a cell phone. She ducked down behind the counter, as not to be seen with an entire pie and a fork in hand, and then she enthusiastically dug in. She could hear the person talking, getting closer to her as he answered the call.

"Hello Mr. President," he answered.

Janet nearly dropped the pie pan when she heard his response.

"Yes, I saw the show. I've already been to the network and now I'm in the Kimberly Cross studio looking for Priscilla and John. They don't seem to be at either location. It looks like the show was filmed from another destination," said Davis.

Janet's fears started to return as she listened to the mysterious conversation.

"I know I told you they wouldn't' get this far, but we still have the General Election and I promise you, neither one will make it as candidates," said Davis.

At that moment, Janet realized she was in the room with the network terrorist. He was working for the President of the United States and he was looking for Priscilla and John. What did he say? He would keep them from becoming presidential candidates? She had to tell someone. She had to see his face. If she stood, he would see her. She couldn't let that happen. It was best he not know she was there. She knew about him, but he didn't know about her.

Janet got an idea. If she let him leave first, she could follow behind him, maybe to an elevator. She would get in with him and get a good look at his face, memorize it, start a conversation and possibly learn something about him.

"Certainly, I understand, and in order for that to happen, we have to locate the contestants. Yes Mr. President, I'm on my way," said Davis. He turned and headed back the way he came in.

Janet was terrified, but she quickly made her way from behind the counter to the dining area. She saw the back of Agent Davis as he exited the cafeteria. She ran to the exit door and slowly opened it to see where he was. On the other side was a long hallway leading to a service elevator. People were walking from corridor to corridor, still talking about the show. Davis made his way to the elevator, pushed the button and waited patiently for it to arrive. Now was her chance. She still hadn't seen his face, but she would if she could get inside the elevator with him.

She took a deep breath, regained her composure and entered the hallway. She stared at the back of the man in front of the elevator, hoping he'd turn around so she could catch a glimpse of his face. Fifteen feet, ten feet, she was getting closer, completely focused on the back of his head, waiting for him to turn around, while people entered and exited the hallway. Five feet, she heard the elevator bell ding, she was almost there, totally focused on the man in front of the elevator. Three feet from the elevator and the door opened.

Bam! All of a sudden, Janet was knocked to the floor by someone entering the hallway. It was Frank Soars, drunk from champagne. He accidentally ran into her on his way to the cafeteria.

Davis entered the elevator, turned and pushed the lobby button. He looked at the two people on the hallway floor and recognized them immediately. Janet looked up and saw his face. She stared intensely at him as the doors slowly closed and she burned his image into her memory.

Finally, the doors closed and he was gone. It all happened so quickly. Janet got to her feet and pulled Frank up.

"Janet Kendrick, where did you go? You're missing a perfectly, wonderful party." Frank brushed himself off, giving the impression that Janet had ran into him.

"Frank, that was him, the terrorist. That was him, did you see him?" Janet was pointing at the elevator.

"The terrorist was a service elevator?" inquired the intoxicated director of programming.

"Frank, listen, I saw him. I heard what he's going to do. He's working for the President," exclaimed Janet.

"What? No, no, no, there is no more terrorist. The show is over." Frank was too drunk to understand.

"Where's Kimberly?" asked Janet.

"She's still at the party, waiting for you," said Frank.

"Come on then, let's go." Janet grabbed Frank by the arm and took him back to the party.

She met with Kimberly and explained what had happened.

Kimberly ordered her security staff to block and monitor all the exits, but it was too late. Davis was no longer at the studio.

The next day brought on the Primary Election and the polls indicated that Mullens and Alden were the people's choice and they had been dubbed America's pre-presidential sweethearts. They looked good together and supported one another, but most of all, they had proved themselves to be reliable candidates. Without a doubt, they would be the next couple occupying the Whitehouse. That was obvious to everyone, including the President.

Agent Davis returned to the Whitehouse and knew his meeting with the President wasn't going to be a pleasant one.

"What happened Davis, are you losing it? I thought I could depend on you." The President scowled as he sat at his desk and read the headlines of the morning newspaper.

"It's not over yet, Mr. President," replied Davis.

The president folded the paper and then slammed it down on the desk.

"No, it's not over Davis. It's just beginning," he shouted. "Because of you, we'll have game show contestants running this country. Because of you, people are altering their lifestyles because of what they saw on a reality TV show. Because of you, this country is going to go to hell."

"Mr. President," Davis calmly interrupted.

"Davis, I expected you to take care of this situation long before the primaries. All you had to do was remove a simple reality television show from the air. You told me you could handle it. No problem, Mr. President, you said. Consider it done." The President picked up the folded paper and waved it in the air and his face started to flush.

"Mr. President," Davis calmly interrupted again.

"And then, due to your inept attempts, not only did you not

succeed, you managed to make that show the most watched and trusted television show in America. I should have pulled you off this assignment a long time ago. You're washed up Davis, finished. You're no good to the agency or the Whitehouse. It's time for you to leave." He was staring at Davis as he shouted.

Agent Davis walked up to the President and stood directly in front of him, eye to eye.

"Before you ramble on old man, I want you to listen to what I have to say." The agent's words came out forcefully to intimidate the leader of our nation.

"I've been with this agency longer than you've held that impressive title of yours. I know things about you and Presidents before you that shouldn't leave the walls of this establishment. If reports of your extra curricular activities ever made it to the media, Mr. President, you'd all be in a lot of trouble. You're no better than the rest of us, hiding your dirty little secrets, trying to keep your job. That's what this is all about, isn't it? You're afraid someone's going to come into your precious political world and rewrite the Constitution, throw out all your old outdated ideas, amendments and policies and make you all look like a bunch of old fools. Don't worry though, Mr. President, because I'm just as much a part of this ridiculous obsolete system as you are, and like you, I'm going to do anything I can to keep it this way. I mean, anything."

The President stepped back without saying a word and looked at Davis. He paused for a moment and then said, "You made your point Davis. I believe you understand the importance of this situation. Therefore, you have one more chance to correct things."

"It's better you don't know what I have planned," said Davis.

"I understand. When do you think you'll have things corrected?" asked the President.

"First, I have to locate the candidates. I'll hang around the television studios. Someone's bound to have some information," said Davis.

"Make friends with that executive producer, what's her name? Janet Kendrick," said the President.

"No, I've got a bad feeling about her. I think she knows more than we want her too," said Davis.

"What do you mean?" the President inquired.

"It was the way she stared at me. This may sound paranoid, but I think she was trying to memorize my face," said Davis.

"Then stay away from her, just do what you have to do," said the President.

"I will, Mr. President," replied Davis.

Agent Davis returned to California the next day. He was a man obsessed. No longer was it just an assignment. Never had he had so much difficulty. Never had he taken so long. Never had a President doubted his performance. He had one more chance and only one more chance to get the job done. The agent was turning into a robot with one mission programmed into his memory. That mission was to eliminate the Independent Presidential Candidates, at any cost.

Chapter Twenty-Seven
The 2012 Presidential Election

Through the month of October, Priscilla and John moved back and forth from Idaho to California, maneuvering between any confrontations that may have existed from the show. All information that may have been leaked to anyone was misleading or completely incorrect as all scheduled appointments were strictly confidential and changed at the last minute. The plan was to have the Independent Political Campaign Headquarters at the network, but in November, at the last minute, Priscilla and John decided to stay in Boise and made Clearwater Cable their campaign headquarters.

It was the day of the General Election and the lines to the voting booths were never ending. The media was playing it up and replaced the phrase "voter's apathy" to "voter's fervor." Registered voters came from everywhere and they consisted of all ages, race and gender. Some people had to wait for hours, causing them to miss half a day of work or school, but that wasn't important. This year, the air was thick with a special kind of political awareness. People actually thought their votes could make a difference.

Mullens and Alden held a landslide lead in the polls and the numbers for the Democratic and Republican parties were at embarrassing record lows. He had only one more chance and he was running out of time. Now that the Independent Candidates has settled, Agent Davis hopped a flight to Boise and was making his way to Clearwater Cable with his soul purpose still coursing through his veins, to eliminate Mullens and Alden before their victory could be announced. He'd make it quick and easy, in and out. He'd simply enter campaign headquarters and blend in with the rest of the people there. Once inside, he'd find a spot where he couldn't be seen and the moment the champagne and balloons began to pop, he'd fire two shots. The first directed at the Independent Presidential Candidate and the second at her Vice President Nominee. The gunfire would be camouflaged by the campaign popping noises and as the two candidates fall to the ground, he'd be on his way out. By the time onlookers figured out their candidates had been shot and killed, he'd be long gone with the result being a Democrat or Republican becoming the next President.

The network and *Millenica* staff and crew members were all volunteering at Clearwater Cable Campaign Headquarters, supporting their Independent Presidential Candidate with the rest of America. Simon was in full costume, dressed as the Political Terminator, as he took pictures with and signed autographs for his loyal fans. Even the corporate officers made it a point to be a part of the festive occasion. They flew to Boise in a private jet with bartenders, a couple of chefs and catered food in tow. Janet, Richard and Simon were on stage standing behind Priscilla and John. Below the stage, Frank, Edward, William, Robert, and Joey all shouted in unison for the candidates to make a speech and then the rest of the people joined in. While this was going on, Agent Davis made his way into the room.

"Speech, speech, speech, speech," roared the crowd.

Priscilla stepped up to the front center of the stage and everyone quieted down. A television camera zoomed in on her as she began to speak.

"Thank you all very much. John and I know that, even though the final numbers haven't been announced yet, we know we're on our way to the Whitehouse."

The crowd let out a cheer and then Priscilla continued.

"You've all let us know how you feel and what you feel is important for this country. Your suggestions have been heard, have been put to work and will be beneficial in making America an influential nation. I honestly believe that we still have a lot of growing to do before we become that nation that inspires other nations. We're still no better than the cavemen that roamed this planet many years ago using fire and clubs to fight for possessions and what they believed in. With technology, we've made the fire more powerful and enhanced the clubs, but we still fight for the same things. Humanity has to begin progressing as quickly as technology. The Earth is our home and it has been very patient with our fighting over the years, but it can't continue. A house where there is no harmony is no longer a home, and everyone, at this time, there is no other planet that we can run away to. Humanity has become the issue! The fighting has got to stop! Without humanity and without this planet, what's the point of war? It's time for us to move up to the next level of humanity, to a world living in harmony."

Everyone clapped and cheered and while Priscilla was giving her speech, Davis found a spot in the room where he couldn't be seen by the crowd.

The General Election was almost over and the landslide lead Mullens and Alden held throughout the day could not be beaten. Priscilla and John stood proudly on the stage waiting for the final numbers to be announced. Simon stood behind the two of them waving to his fans. Richard and Janet stood behind Simon, responsible for creating this presidential victory.

All of a sudden, from up on the stage, Janet could see Davis. The way he was positioned, he couldn't be seen by the crowd below, but he could be seen from the people on the stage and since nobody knew who he was, he appeared to be another face in the crowd.

That is, except to Janet. The memory of him standing in the elevator still burned in her memory. She pulled Richard and Simon off to the side and tried to warn them.

"That's him, that's the man I heard talking to the President. He's here to kill Priscilla and John," she exclaimed.

"What?" asked Richard.

Simon looked in the direction Janet was pointing and saw the C.I.A. agent. Davis saw Janet on the stage pointing him out and knew he'd been recognized. There was nothing left for him to do but follow through with his plan. He reached inside his coat pocket and pulled out a gun.

Simon saw what he was doing and visions of the John F. Kennedy assassination filled his head. He couldn't let it happen again. Another great leader wasn't going to be eliminated by the bullet of an assassin. He saw Davis taking aim at Priscilla and he knew it was up to him to save her. He lunged forward and tried to push her out of the way just as the gun went off.

Janet tried to stop Simon, but Richard grabbed onto her and held her tightly to keep her out of the line of fire. Simon and Priscilla both fell to the floor.

"Somebody get that man!" shouted Richard as he pointed at Davis and held tightly onto Janet. Edward and William immediately sprang into action, kicked the gun out of his hand and wrestled Davis to the floor, while the rest of the crowd waited to see what was happening on stage. Janet looked at the crowed as they looked up at her. Richard was still holding her and she couldn't move. She looked down at the floor and saw blood flowing toward her, forming a small pool by her feet. She looked over at Priscilla and Simon on the floor, the blood flowing from their motionless bodies.

"Somebody call an ambulance!" shouted Frank. Robert and Joey sprang into action. Robert called an ambulance while Joey called the police.

Then, Priscilla began to move and was unaware of what happened. She had hit her head when she landed on the floor and it momentarily knocked her out. John ran over and helped her to her feet and then escorted her to safety.

Simon still did not move. He had been shot in the chest and from the amount of blood he was losing, it looked serious. Richard saw the blood and ran to his friend's side to see what he could do. He rolled him over on his back to see how badly Simon was hurt.

"Simon, speak to me, Simon. Oh my God, you're bleeding so much." Richard ripped the sleeve from his shirt and pressed it against Simon's wound. He responded by opening his eyes and tried to speak, but he was too weak and was having difficulty breathing. Richard told him to rest and wait for the ambulance.

Janet stood alone on the stage, holding back her tears looking at the pool of blood next to her feet. Why hadn't she seen that it was Simon's blood in her premonition? She could have warned him. Robert saw her standing alone and went to her side.

"Ms. Kendrick, an ambulance is on the way. I think it would be better if you sat down." Robert took Janet by the arm and escorted her off the stage. As they passed Simon, she saw the amount of blood he was losing and she began to cry. Once off the stage, Robert held her in his arms and let her cry on his shoulder.

"Richard, is Priscilla alright?" asked Simon. He struggled to speak.

"Yes, she's fine. Maybe a small bump on the head, that's all. You saved her life. You really shouldn't be talking Simon, just rest," said Richard. Simons' blood was coating his hand.

"We did it Richard, we really did it," said Simon.

"Simon, please just rest. An ambulance is going to be here any moment," said Richard in desperation.

"They won the election. Priscilla is President of the United States," Simon held a painful smile as he spoke.

He knew where the conversation was heading, but he didn't want to let Simon go. The cloth he was holding was now saturated with blood and the young college student's eyes began to water knowing there was nothing more he could do.

"That's right, you got Priscilla to the Whitehouse and you saved her life. You saved the life of the President of the United States Simon. Not too many people can achieve a goal twice in one lifetime, but you did it," he said.

"You've been a good friend to me Mr. Weeks. I want you to know how much I appreciate that." Simon winced as he felt a sharp pain in his chest. He knew he didn't have much more time, but he had one more thing to say.

"Thank you Richard." Simon squeezed Richard's hand and then closed his eyes. His grip disappeared and Richard was left gripping Simon's hand.

Richard realized that Simon had just passed away and he was no longer in any pain.

"Simon, don't go." He spoke quietly as he cried.

Joey was watching Richard from the crowd below and he saw what happened. He went and kneeled next to Richard and noticed that Simon wasn't breathing. The time had come for Joey to support his best friend and help him through his painful loss.

"Richard, are you alright?" he asked softly.

Richard didn't speak. He just stared at Simon with tears coming from his eyes, still holding his hand and the cloth to his wound as if it was going to somehow bring him back to life.

"Richard, the Professor's gone. Let him go," said Joey.

Richard looked at Joey, but still didn't speak.

"He's in a better place now, and he's happy," said Joey. "You know, I think he knew he was going to do this all along. He kept saying that he wanted to create the next President of the United States, and that he did. He also kept saying that he wanted to retire after that. He did that too. In his heart, he knew what he had to do. He just didn't know what destiny had planned for him until it presented itself. Think about it, he went from being a college professor, to being a television star, and now he's a hero."

Richard looked at Simon and with a teary smile he said, "What a grand exit."

"What a grand exit indeed. The ambulance is almost here. You don't mind if I wait here with you?" asked Joey.

"Sure," said Richard.

The police and the ambulance arrived at about the same time. Simon's body was placed on a gurney and taken to the hospital. Frank and Richard went along to answer any questions the hospital may have had. Agent Davis was taken away in handcuffs and the police received statements from witnesses in the crowd. It didn't look too good for the C.I.A. agent, but he trusted the President would take care of him.

Robert took Janet back to her hotel room where he sat and talked about the events of the show. His main purpose was to take away the guilt she was holding for all the unfortunate incidents that occurred to the contestants as well as Simon's death. After a while, they started talking about next year's show.

"So, what do you have planned?" asked Robert.

"Nothing like this again. I don't think I can take it," said Janet.

"Sure you can. Besides, Priscilla and John are going to need a lot of help restructuring that Whitehouse. I think we can assist them in that department," said Robert.

"How?" asked Janet.

"There are a lot of important political positions that could use a little enhancing. I say, why not ask the people where our government still needs improvements and take it from there," said Robert.

Janet sat silently for a moment looking at Robert going over what he had said.

"So *Millenica* goes on, year after year, asking the people for their ideas on how to improve our government. We give them what they want, until we've completely restructured the Whitehouse and our political process," said Janet.

"And, with all the changes we need, just to catch up to this millennium, this show is going to be on the air for a long time," laughed Robert.

"And, with every presidential election, we continue to create the people's choice for the Independent Presidential Candidate," said Janet.

"That's right, we don't want those Republicans, Democrats and previous Independents getting lazy," said Robert.

Janet went to the window and looked outside.

"So, *Millenica* was supposed to happen?" she asked.

"That's right Ms. Kendrick, and now it's time for us to put it to good use," said Robert.

Janet turned and looked back at Robert with a sad expression.

"Who's going to replace Simon? Who can be the next Political Terminator?" she asked.

"I know just the person. He'll be perfect. All I have to do is make a phone call to Clearwater Cable to get the ball rolling," said Robert.

Chapter Twenty-Eight
In Memory Of

A hero's funeral was held for Simon and the number of people who attended was immense. It was televised on every channel and ran for days. Tabloid magazines held captions like "The Political Terminator Gets Terminated," while the more respectable news magazines ran captions like "From Host To Hero" and "The Legend Of Griswald." In any event, all articles portrayed him as the hero who saved the President of the United States.

Priscilla and John took their places in the Whitehouse. They looked good together and the differences in their nationalities brought a new sense of awareness to the people. It made them realize what this country was all about and what made it strong. As promised, Priscilla hired the contestants from the show to be her Whitehouse staff, and she had them immediately start working on her fire year plan to improve the country. As she worked with them on the project, John focused on the security of America. They made an excellent Whitehouse team.

Agent Davis was placed under arrest and waited for his day in court. His ace in the hole, the former President, was under investigation for political deceit and corruption. It looked like the two would have a good chance of sharing the same prison cell.

It was the end of spring at Boise State University, and the rainy weather was beginning to let up. The sun was making more of an appearance causing flowers to bloom, grass to grow, and leaves to flourish. A statue of Simon had been created and was placed outside his old classroom, near the window he looked out on a daily basis. A small dedication was being held that included Frank, Janet, Robert, Richard, Joey, Edward, William, the Dean of the university, and Kimberly Cross. Everyone brought up accounts they had with Simon, the Professor, and the Political Terminator. Richard made a final comment mentioning how Simon's statue would be a constant reminder throughout the decades of what amazing things people can do when they believe in themselves and their dreams. At that time, Joey went over to Richard.

"Speaking of dreams, what do you have planned for this year?" asked Joey.

"I guess, go back to school and finish where I left off," said Richard.

"A while back, I got a call from someone who thought it might be a good idea if you finish where Simon left off," Joey was looking over at Robert as he spoke. "I told him I thought it was a good idea. What do you think?"

"I don't understand what you're asking. What do you mean, finish where Simon left off?" asked Richard.

"Richard, we want to keep *Millenica*. We feel that if used properly, it will do great things. You were the inspiration of the show," said Janet.

"That's right young man, and I remember watching your class project tape. You were quite an impressive host," said Frank.

"Wait a minute, you want me to be the next host of *Millenica*?" asked Richard.

"You'd be perfect," said Robert.

"And don't forget, we have a new TV station in Boise now. You could do shows from here whenever you get homesick," said Joey. "I'm thinking maybe a holiday special."

"That's something you don't know yet," said Frank. "We've made Clearwater Cable a sister site for the network in California. Robert and Joey are in charge of station programming."

"With the money he made from the deal, Brophy took a long vacation and is traveling around the world. Before he left, he put me and Robert in charge. I told you I was going to eventually own this station one day," said Joey.

Richard couldn't believe what he was hearing and didn't know what to say.

"Come on Richard, say you'll do it. History just repeated itself and you were a big part of it," said William.

"And now that we've started over, you've got to keep the momentum going," said Edward.

"If someone knew Simon the most, it was you," said Kimberly. "He trusted you enough to make you his manager. He trusted you like a son. He believed in you as much as you believed in him."

"You're the only one worthy of that position Richard," said Joey.

Everyone stood looking at Richard, waiting for him go give an answer. Finally, he turned around and looked up at Simon's statute.

"Maybe they're right Simon," he said. "You were there from the beginning. You looked so nervous when I told you I was putting my class project on TV, but you didn't say no. If it weren't for you, *Millenica* wouldn't have happened and Priscilla and John wouldn't be in the Whitehouse. I know I'll never be as good as you, but I think I'm going to give it a try. If you really believed in me, I know you'll be there with me. So don't let them make me look stupid, okay?"

"Does this mean you'll do it?" asked Janet.

"I don't know how I'm going to break this to my parents, but yes, I'll do it," said Richard.

"This calls for a celebration and I know the perfect place. Everyone, follow me," said Joey.

They all went off to celebrate, full of energy, excitement and enthusiasm. When they were gone, a ray of sunshine streamed down from between the clouds and shined on Simon's statute.

The millennium pilgrims found their way to the Whitehouse using *Millenica* as their vessel to get there. Their new goal, to protect the planet, nurture humanity and create a country that will inspire other countries. Priscilla said it best during her winning presentation speech.

"Before the sun grows dark and cold. Before a stray asteroid crashes into the face of our planet. Before the Earth's molten core hardens and turns the world we know into a vast wasteland. Before all that, what is the fate of this world and humanity?

"The time has come for everyone to stop thinking separately as countries and continents and start thinking as a world united. It's distressing to think that, because of politics, religious beliefs and greed, we the people will be the cause of our own destruction as well as destroying this beautiful planet we were given the opportunity to nurture."

"We have the power and technology to make positive changes for ourselves and this planet. The question is, will we?"

Printed in the United States
85659LV00002B/49/A